Earth's the Right Place for Love

Earth's
the
Right Place
for
Love

A NOVEL

Elizabeth Berg

RANDOM HOUSE  NEW YORK

Published in the United States by Random House, an imprint and division of Penguin Random House LLC, New York.

RANDOM HOUSE and the HOUSE colophon are registered trademarks of Penguin Random House LLC.

LIBRARY OF CONGRESS CATALOGING-IN-PUBLICATION DATA
Names: Berg, Elizabeth, author.
Title: Earth's the right place for love : a novel / Elizabeth Berg.
Other titles: Earth is the right place for love
Description: First edition. | New York : Random House, [2023]
Identifiers: LCCN 2022010405 (print) | LCCN 2022010406 (ebook) |
ISBN 9780593446799 (hardback ; acid-free paper) | ISBN 9780593446812 (ebook)
Subjects: LCGFT: Novels.
Classification: LCC PS3552.E6996 E18 2023 (print) | LCC PS3552.E6996 (ebook) |
DDC 813/.54—dc23/eng/20220303
LC record available at https://lccn.loc.gov/2022010405
LC ebook record available at https://lccn.loc.gov/2022010406

Printed in the United States of America on acid-free paper

randomhousebooks.com

2 4 6 8 9 7 5 3 1

FIRST EDITION

Frontispiece photo courtesy of iStock/ImagoRB

Book design by Carole Lowenstein

To Robert Michael Noerper
It's about time

I'd like to get away from earth awhile
And then come back to it and begin over.
May no fate willfully misunderstand me
And half grant what I wish and snatch me away
Not to return. Earth's the right place for love:
I don't know where it's likely to go better.

—from "Birches" by Robert Frost

Earth's the Right Place for Love

Mason, Missouri
Winter 2016

ARTHUR MOSES BELIEVES it is not a terrible thing to think that you may be dying. He is eighty-five years old and in his own house, in his own bed, in the town he has lived in all his life. He sleeps comfortably enough and is visited by people he loves.

He waits for small things now. Snow falling, slow and waltzy. A door opening, then closing. The ring of a spoon against a mixing bowl, the warm smell of cake. Rose petals dropping onto the nightstand. Black clouds parting like curtains to reveal the stars. And always, the sound of the train whistle. That sound brings back memories of the spring he was sixteen, when he came into life for the second time.

Chapter 1

SOMETIMES ARTHUR SNUCK out of his house at night. He didn't go anywhere, just sat on the back steps outside the kitchen door. Here, he pondered things that were too big to fit inside the bedroom he shared with his older brother, Frank. Even in sleep, Frank seemed a large and nearly incandescent presence. A person like Frank didn't leave a lot of room for a guy like Arthur, unintentional though it was. And Arthur didn't mind, really. Being outside was a reminder to him that there was a place for all things, and, in that respect, didn't everything have equal value? Off to the side in the backyard, for instance, were daisies. Up above was the majesty of the moon and the stars and the rings of Saturn that he knew were there whether he could see them or not. And here, sitting on the steps in his pajamas, was Arthur, feeling that he was right where he should be. For him, life was like a gift perpetually ready for the opening. Cockeyed optimist,

Frank called him, but Arthur wasn't sure he was cock-eyed at all.

He wished that a certain someone would care to hear his thoughts. Hear and understand them. He guessed that everyone came to a time in their life when they started to be aware of a specific kind of loneliness. It reminded him of filmstrips he'd seen in science class: seeds buried in the earth and then sprouting, growing what looked like arms reaching out. On the rough concrete beneath him, he traced out the letters to her name: NOLA. Then he went back inside.

The next day, after school let out, Arthur went again to the chain-link fence near the front entrance of the high school and waited, hoping to catch a glimpse of Nola McCollum. He'd been doing this for several days now. Sometimes he smashed down dirt clods, a poor attempt to seem like he was doing something. More often he stood sideways, as though his attention were taken up by something off in the distance.

If she did not come out, he knew she had stayed after for one reason or another: a club meeting, cheerleading practice, rehearsal for a concert or a play. But if she did come out, he watched as she descended the steps and turned left toward home.

Nola was very popular, and almost always with a group of friends and admirers; Arthur once counted twelve people with her. But today she came out by herself, and everything in Arthur ratcheted up to high alert.

She was looking down and smiling, seemingly lost in thought. He liked the brown tweed skirt and yellow sweater she was wearing, and the way her coat was open to the mild April day. It was a chance for him finally to talk to her alone, to say . . . Well, that was the problem. To say what? She was mythical to him, barely real. But there she was, carrying books and wearing socks and shoes like everyone else. Just as she passed Arthur, the wind lifted her black hair and blew it across her face. Arthur swallowed around the boulder in his throat and called out, "Hey, Nola!"

She moved her hair aside and turned to look at him. "Oh, *hi,* Arthur!"

He walked up to her, his heart banging in his chest.

"I'm glad to see you," she said.

"Oh!" he said. "Well, that's nice!"

"I've been meaning to ask you if you could do me a favor." She turned her head and regarded him sideways, her eyebrows raised. Was she *flirting* with him?

"Sure! What is it?"

"Well . . . it's just that, like a lot of other girls, I have a crush on your brother."

Arthur's heart sank. "Frank?"

"Uh-huh. Gosh, I'm embarrassed to ask you, but do you think there's any chance . . . Can I give you my number to give to him?"

"Yeah, I guess so. Sure."

She pulled out a piece of paper and a pencil and wrote down the number. When she looked up, she smiled at him. "I'm probably being foolish," she said. She folded the paper and handed it to him.

Arthur shoved it deep into his pocket. "You know what?" he said. "I think it's a good idea to let someone know you care about them. They might not be aware." He tried to look meaningfully into her eyes.

But Nola only said, "You're so nice to say that. Thanks for not making fun of me."

"I would never make fun of you, Nola."

She hiked up her shoulders. "Well, that's that!"

"Right," Arthur said.

"See you," she said, and her gaze lingered on him for a moment. Then she walked away.

Arthur watched her go. It was awfully sweet, the way she'd said, "See you." And he thought she'd looked at him in a way she never had before. Maybe she'd never really noticed him before, but now something could have been planted in her brain. Oh, sure, she'd approached him wanting him to give her number to his brother, but wasn't it possible she'd been aware that she was giving it to Arthur, too?

As Arthur started to head home, someone else came out of the building: Harvey Guldorp, a boy even more invisible in their sophomore class than Arthur believed he himself was. Harvey was wearing a winter cap with the ear flaps down and the chin strap firmly affixed, despite the mild weather. "Hey Arthur," Harvey said, "why are you always hanging around after school lets out?" "Ferret," some people called Harvey, for the way he was always finding things out. "What are you waiting for?"

"Nothing," Arthur said.

So far, it wasn't a lie.

"You want to come over and read Green Hornet comics?" Harvey asked. "I got some new ones."

Arthur didn't. But he knew enough about rejection to say, "Sure." And so he moved away from his fantasy of making headway with Nola and into the reality of Harvey Guldorp's invitation to read comics in what Arthur imagined to be Harvey's messy bedroom, overheated and no doubt smelling of Vicks VapoRub.

Chapter 2

ARTHUR'S BROTHER, FRANK, was eighteen and Arthur thought he knew just about everything there was to know, including how to get under their father's skin. Arthur didn't understand why Frank provoked their dad so, but sometimes it was fun. Tonight, after they went to bed, Frank told Arthur about his latest idea.

"I don't know," Arthur said. "He might not think it's funny. He might get mad."

"It's just a little prank."

"I don't know," Arthur said again.

Frank said, "Come on, Arthur, you've got to learn to take some chances!"

That was true, so Arthur listened with Frank until they heard their parents climbing the creaky steps for bed. "Okay, here goes," Frank whispered. He quietly lined up four shoes along the top of the cracked-open bedroom door. Arthur pulled the covers up to his nose. Now all that was left was to decide who should yell.

"I think you should do it," Frank whispered. "He always comes flying up if he thinks you're in trouble. If I do it, he'll just think I'm funning."

"I'm not doing it," Arthur whispered back. "You're the one who thought of this."

"Precisely. I thought of it, so you execute it."

He had a point, Arthur supposed, and he began making a moaning sound like he was having a bad dream: "*Ohhhhhhhh, ohhhhhh!*"

"No," Frank whispered. "It needs to be more like an *emergency*." Forgetting himself, he demonstrated with a bloodcurdling scream. Arthur felt the hairs on the back of his neck rise, even though he was right there with his brother, knowing it was all fake.

It worked, of course. Here came the thundering steps of their father up the stairs to their attic bedroom. He banged open the door, and the shoes fell on his head. Arthur burst out laughing while Frank feigned sleep. "Sorry," Arthur said. "I just thought it would be funny. You're not hurt, are you? Are you hurt?"

Their father stood there. The quiet was awful. Arthur hoped he hadn't been drinking; that always made things worse. He looked from one of the beds to the other. Then he flung Frank's covers back, grabbed him by the neck of his pajamas, and yanked at him. "Downstairs," he said.

Arthur sat up. "I did it," he said. "Wait! I'm the one. He was sleeping!"

He didn't mind sacrificing himself because their dad went easier on him. When Arthur did something wrong, he only got yelled at or maybe a quick swat. Sixteen years old and he was always having trouble with anemia and ear infections and rashes and whatnot. That saved him from their father's anger. It was why Arthur didn't mind being sick so much. That and Frank playing cards with him, the times Arthur had to lie in bed all day. They played cards, they played Monopoly, they talked about girls, and Arthur shared the meals he got delivered to him on a tray because Frank loved sick-people food: chicken soup and ginger ale and custard with nutmeg grated on top.

"Into the barn," Arthur's father said to Frank, referring to the tiny structure in the backyard that housed the chickens and their little bay horse, Grimy, who still pulled the milk cart. Their dad refused to get a truck, saying that the milk-delivery business was coming to an end, anyway.

Arthur knew what would happen in the barn. He knew Frank would suffer far beyond the seriousness of the crime. It was always that way; it was like their father had something against his firstborn. Knowing that, you'd think Frank would have stopped with the shenanigans. But he didn't. He dug in deeper. But now, once again, he had gone too far.

Arthur heard the slap of flesh on flesh. "Stop it, Pop," he heard Frank say, all the way down the stairs. "Gee whiz, *stop* it!" Arthur knew Frank would be holding his hands in the air above his head, trying to ward off the blows.

"Eugene!" their mother called from where she stood out in the hall. "Don't!" She'd be looking down, one hand on the railing, the other clutching her robe tightly against her neck. "Eugene, can't you just . . . Eu*gene*!"

Arthur bent his head down, closed his eyes tightly, and held still. He kept on listening, though he didn't really want to. He heard the back door open and slam shut. He flung off his covers and went to the window to watch as their dad half dragged, half pushed his brother across the yard and into the barn. He thought, *Frank is getting too old for this.*

Frank had a lot of hair on his chest, his voice was deep, and he was as tall as their dad. Arthur stared at the closed door of the barn and thought, *One of these days, one of them is going to kill the other.* He returned to his bed and sat on the edge, waiting for it to be over, his hands clasped tightly between his knees. He guessed he should have tried to stop his brother, but there was never any stopping Frank.

After a few minutes, he heard the back door open again, and he heard his brother on the way upstairs, followed by the heavier, slower steps of their father.

"You okay?" Arthur whispered when Frank came into their room.

"Sure I am." Frank got in bed and turned away from Arthur. The moon shone through the window and Arthur thought about how it was like that: anything could happen and still the moon would rise.

After a while, he fell asleep. He'd wanted to stay up with Frank; he could tell his brother was awake, staring at the wall. But Arthur fell asleep, and in the morning when he woke up, there was Frank sitting on the side of his bed tying his shoes and grinning over at Arthur like nothing had happened. "I'm going down for breakfast," he said. "I'm not going to leave *you* much."

He went downstairs and Arthur heard their mother talking to him like a minister talks to one of the fallen: disappointed, but still kind. "You can have more sugar than that, Frank. Here. Take more. Sit up straight, son."

Arthur washed up, dressed, and made his bed. Then he made Frank's bed so his brother wouldn't get in trouble for not doing it. He pulled the blankets up tight. Fluffed the pillow. Fluffed it better. Before he went downstairs, he looked again out the window at the barn, a different building, somehow, in the daylight. He thought of his brother in there last night, furious but resigned.

Arthur grabbed his schoolbooks and headed down to the kitchen, which would be warm and empty of their father, who, at mealtimes, tucked a napkin into the top of his shirt, rolled up his sleeves, and chewed his food like he was taking something out on it.

Frank was gone. He'd left Arthur plenty, including the toast he hadn't touched, which his mother now slid onto Arthur's plate. "I don't know why he is in such an all-fired rush to get to school these days," she said.

"He probably just wants to be outside," Arthur said, in a way that he thought would cover for Frank.

His mother turned around from the stove, where she had begun scrambling eggs. "Outside? He's not outside when he's in school."

"I mean on the way," Arthur said. "You know, on the way to school. He's outside, walking there."

"Well, Arthur. Use your head. Do you have to walk to school to be outside? He could sit out on the front steps to wait for you, and he'd be outside. You could walk to school together like you used to do."

"Ma?"

"What?"

He pointed to the pan. He didn't like his eggs over-done. He liked them very soft, and his mother was glad to accommodate him.

The difference between his mother and his father was something to contemplate. He couldn't come right out and ask his mother, "Why are you with him?" But it was something he thought about.

One night, when they were lying in their beds and talking, Arthur had asked Frank about that. Frank said, "Well, the way I see it, there's only one person for everyone. And when you find them, that's that. Good or bad, that's that. You fall in love with your heart, not with your brain, so sometimes things don't work out so perfectly." A while later, Arthur heard him say, "It's written in the stars."

Arthur wondered if his brother was talking in his sleep. "Frank," he whispered. "Are you awake?"

"What are you talking about? Obviously I'm awake."

"I thought you were dreaming. You were talking some kind of mumbo jumbo about the stars."

"It's not mumbo jumbo. It's fate." Frank yawned. "I know someone who knows a lot about this. She's a fortune teller, a real one. I'll take you to meet her sometime. She'll tell you your future."

"She doesn't know my future," Arthur had said. "How would *she* know?"

"Arthur, what *you* don't know is a lot. *There are more things in heaven and earth, Horatio, than are dreamt of in your philosophy.*"

Arthur hated it when Frank did that: changed his voice to some lofty tone and spat out something that barely sounded English. It was like when Arthur would try and try to fix something, and Frank would waltz in and fix it lickety-split. At least he didn't say anything at such times. He'd just do it and walk away. But it still got Arthur's goat.

The reason Frank went to school early was because he was in love with his English teacher. And she was in love with him. That was what Frank had told Arthur. For a while now, Frank had been staying after school to be with her. Arthur figured that now he was going to start adding in time before school started as well.

They had been on their way home from school a few weeks before when Frank had told Arthur about this. He'd stopped walking and said, "Hold up a minute."

Arthur had waited. He thought maybe Frank had spotted someone he wanted to talk to. Frank had a million friends.

But it was Arthur Frank wanted to talk to. He said, "You know Miss Anker, right?" His voice was different. Nervous-sounding.

"Sure," Arthur said. Everybody knew Miss Anker. It was her first year there and all the kids knew about her within a few hours of her arrival. She had long red hair that seemed to throw off sparks. Her eyes were a clear, nearly unnatural green. She was so pretty it could make you feel bad. The boys looked at her and felt sick. The girls looked at her and felt angry. She had a red dress with white polka dots she wore sometimes that put everybody on edge. Sometimes a bunch of girls would talk about her at recess, huddled in a corner of the playground, buzzing like bees: *she, she, she.* But plenty of them were suddenly trying to wear scarves around their necks the way she did.

Frank had told Arthur that on his first day in the class-room with Miss Anker, she'd asked, "Who can give me an example of a declarative sentence?" and he hadn't even raised his hand when he said, "I do."

"I *do*," she'd repeated, as he'd known she would, and after that, he told Arthur, he'd just slunk down in his seat with his arms crossed and smiled at her.

"How about some other examples?" she'd asked the class, but Frank said at that point he'd stopped listening and begun scheming. He was pretty darned good-looking himself. And he excelled in English. Two for two. And in the grand scheme of things, their age difference was mini-mal.

When Frank had confessed his feelings for Miss Anker to Arthur, he'd also said that last week he'd skipped bas-ketball practice to go to her house. She'd invited him there. She thought he was an awfully good writer, and she wanted to help him with a story she was going to submit to some magazine for him. They didn't work too much on his story, though, Frank had said. And he'd told Arthur they'd gone far enough that he knew she didn't dye her hair. It took Arthur a while to get it.

Arthur hadn't known what to do. He'd felt deeply embarrassed. He started walking quickly away from Frank, outraged at him. And at her. That wasn't what teachers were supposed to do with their students! Frank caught up to him and said, "Come on, I'm near enough a grown-up. Soon as I graduate, I'm going to marry her."

Arthur had said nothing the rest of the way home. He was thinking about how two years ago George Hashler, who was seventeen, had run off with his mother's housekeeper, who was *ages* older than he was. George's mother wouldn't come out of the house for a month, she was so mortified. So Arthur knew these things happened; his mother told him they were called May-December romances. He'd just never thought such a thing would happen to his brother, who could have his pick of any of the girls at their high school.

When they got home that day, before they went into the house, Frank had said, "You're not going to tell on me, are you?"

Arthur had just looked at him. Of course he wasn't going to tell on him. But he was plenty worried. There was playing with fire, and then there was setting yourself on fire.

Chapter 3

O N SATURDAYS, FRANK had a job bagging groceries at Clauson's Ready Mart, and Arthur did odd jobs for the neighbors. Frank had already left for work when Arthur heard his mother call up for him to come down right away: Mrs. Trentino had a job for him, and she wanted him there as soon as possible.

Arthur spent a long time getting dressed, and he did not exactly fly down the stairs. He did things for Mrs. Trentino every now and then, and he didn't much care for her. The old man had been great; he would come out and play stickball with the kids on the block, wheezing out his old man laugh past a cigar clamped between his teeth. "You think you're something?" he'd say. "Huh? You think you're something? You watch." There was never much of anything to watch, though. He was just an old man pretending to be young again. His pants would be holding on for dear life; the guy was awfully thin. Arthur never saw him in anything but a white shirt and dark pants. He used to be a traveling salesman, and every time he came home for the weekend, he would drive slowly down the street, throwing hard candy out his car window. All the kids would hustle. Arthur would trade Frank his root-beer barrels for Frank's butterscotch. Mr. Trentino was fun; he *thought* of things. But he'd been gone for a few years, and now Mrs. Trentino sat at her window all day looking for someone to yell at. "Boy!" *Knock-knock-knock* on the window. "You there! Put the newspaper on the *stoop*! What do you think, you put the paper on the *stoop*!"

Arthur ate some cornflakes, and his mother told him to be sure to go to Mrs. Trentino's first. After that, he could go to his regular job, helping Mrs. Crawford with her garden; his mother had called to tell her he'd be by later than usual today.

Arthur came outside into a bright spring day, warm enough that you didn't need a jacket, though his mother had insisted he wear one, as usual. She was right, he guessed. He figured he'd always be weak in the health department. He wished that weren't so, and he wished too that his ears didn't stick out. He wished he were tall, dark, and handsome, not gawky, shy, and plain; he disliked his boring brown eyes and hair, to say nothing of the cowlick he never could tame. He felt like the guy in the backs of the comics who other guys kicked sand at. He *could* make girls smile, and sometimes they called out hello to him at school when they passed in the halls. Arthur bragged on that once to Frank—the way the girls initiated the greeting—but Frank said all that meant was that they found him safe. "What's wrong with that?" Arthur asked, and Frank said he'd come to see what was wrong with it. It was like the way Frank warned Arthur against being seen as too "sweet." But it seemed to Arthur that what you had to watch out for was the opposite: a kind of ready meanness that seemed easier to achieve than kindness; Arthur didn't know why.

He walked slowly down the street, running a stick along the picket fences he passed. It reminded him of the *clickety-clack* of the trains on the tracks, the sound of someone going somewhere, though he himself didn't really want to go anywhere. He liked the familiarity of the things he passed on the neighborhood streets: the arrangements of rocking chairs on front porches, the laundry on the lines out back. When he walked downtown, he liked going past the five-and-dime, with everything from baby dolls to toilet plungers displayed in the front window. He liked watching the women walk primly down the sidewalk with their purses and gloves and hats and high heels. From the diner, the enticing smell of fried onions reached all the way out to the sidewalk.

Arthur liked seeing the butcher, who made his bloody apron less gruesome by his friendly smile and boisterous greetings, and he liked seeing that butcher hoist up a pot roast as though it were a trophy, trying to win the approval of a fussy housewife. He liked watching the kittens in the window of the pet store pounce on one another. The barbershop kept its door propped halfway open, so you could see all the guys sitting there wearing what looked like big bibs. Arthur liked when he heard the church bells pealing, the resonance so deep he could feel it in his chest. He stopped walking for a moment whenever that happened. It was like a moment of church outside of the church.

It was interesting to see who was waiting for the bus, and the way the men sitting on the bench with their legs crossed folded their newspapers just so. Whenever he walked past the car dealership, he hoped Mr. Albenesius would be out smoking a cigarette with his foot propped up on the bumper of one of the cars he'd labeled CREAM PUFF!

Most of all, Arthur liked how the fields started at the edge of town. There the sky opened up and you could see the tall grasses and hear the whispering sound of the wind blowing through them. Redwing blackbirds gathered to roost on a certain branch every evening at sunset. They would line up all in a row and chatter, as though debriefing one another about their day. Arthur guessed this was what home meant: that you walked all over town and everywhere you looked made you think, *Yup*.

He passed a couple where the man had his arm around his girl; the girl was giggling, and she left a trail of sweet perfume. He thought of Nola, about her phone number hidden away in his desk drawer. He hadn't given the number to Frank, but he himself had not yet had the courage to call her. He wondered if she really was the one for him; if his fate had been decided when it came to love. He wouldn't mind, if that were so. Nola Corrine, the Beauty Queen. That's what he called her. She wasn't the prettiest one in the whole school; that was blond-headed Tess McGraw, who was one of Nola's friends. But Nola had a way about her, something that Arthur couldn't describe but felt helplessly drawn to. He guessed she could do just about any ordinary thing and he would think it was something special. Once he was walking a ways behind her and her group from school, and they all were sharing a bag of peanuts in their shells. Arthur saw Nola stop, crouch down, and offer a peanut to a squirrel that was on the boulevard. She was so patient, the way she waited for it to come over and take it from her hand. Her friends stood waiting for her, bored, until she waved them on. Then she caught up to them, and Arthur thought she believed the pleasure of the exchange had been hers alone. Not so.

When Arthur rang Mrs. Trentino's bell, she opened the door so fast Arthur figured she must have been standing there waiting for him. "Morning!" he said.

He felt her sizing him up as though she'd never seen him before. He guessed he'd passed inspection because she stepped to the side and said, "All right, come on, follow me." She looked over her shoulder at him. "You want some cookies first?"

"No, thank you. I just had breakfast."

"After, then," she said, and Arthur thought, *Nope, not then, either.* He'd had her cookies before, and he thought this must be the recipe: *Get some sawdust. Add water. Bake it.*

He followed her into the dining room, where he saw piles and piles of fabric laid out. They covered the large table, and many stacks were almost as high as his head.

"What we're going to do here is pack this all up," she said. "And then I want you to put the bags on my front porch. Neatly. Someone will come and pick them up later this afternoon."

"Okay," Arthur said. This would be easy enough. She had a stack of grocery bags on the table that he figured were meant for the fabric to be put in. He wondered why she couldn't do all this herself, then reasoned that she might have trouble carrying the loaded-up bags to the porch. And she might not be a very good packer; a lot of people weren't, and she might need his help with allocation. Allocation and distribution, that would be his department. Logistics. His dad said that if he'd been able to serve in the war, he would have wanted to be one of those guys: first in, last out. But he was 4-F on account of flat feet with corresponding back pain, something you were well advised not to mention.

Mrs. Trentino snapped a paper bag in the air to open it.

"You know why I'm giving all this away?" she asked.

"No, ma'am."

"Because I can't see to sew anymore." With this she lifted her chin and her mouth tightened.

"Oh. Well, that's . . . I'm awful sorry."

"Never mind, it'll happen to you, too; your eyes will go someday. It's part of getting old. Your eyes will go, your ears, and plenty of other things, too."

Arthur nodded.

She stared at him, the open bag in her hand. "You don't know much of anything, though, do you?"

"Guess not." Arthur could feel color creeping up into his face. He knew some stuff, all right!

She turned to the table. "All right, let's get cracking."

Arthur opened a bag and picked up half of a big pile.

"What are you doing?" Mrs. Trentino asked.

"Putting the cloth in the bag. It's supposed to go in here, right?"

"One piece at a time!"

"Well, I think it might go faster if I—"

"Excuse me. Excuse me! You didn't come over here to tell me how to do this job. I'm not paying you to tell me *how* to do this. I'm paying you to *help* me do it the way *I* want it done."

"Yes, ma'am." He swallowed anything else he might have wanted to say. But he was thinking, *After I put that last bag on the porch, I'll never work for you again.*

He put a few pieces in the bag, one by one, Mrs. Trentino's eyes squinty on him the whole time. When he picked up a light-blue fabric with little white polka dots, she said, "Hold it right there!" and came around to his side of the table. They'd been facing each other across a wide expanse, each of them at one end of the fully open table, but now she was right beside him. He saw how short she was; she couldn't have been more than five feet. He could look down at the part in her hair. She smelled like toast and coffee and ironed things.

She took the folded piece of fabric from him and unfurled it. "You know what I made out of this?"

"No, ma'am."

"Well, I made a summer dress, with the skirt cut on the bias. It had no sleeves, but it had little ruffles at the shoulders, pretty as can be." She thrust it into Arthur's hands. "Feel how light that fabric is!"

"Sure is."

"You can imagine how that dress moved on me. All those years ago."

"Yes, ma'am."

"All right, fold it back up, then," she said. "Neatly."

He started to fold it but she snatched it away again and held it up before her like it was a mirror she was looking into. "I'll never see this fabric again. And the dress is long gone. And here I don't even have a picture of me in it. I *did* have one, because it was a beautiful dress, prettiest dress I ever did make, and my husband took a picture of me in it the first time I wore it. I asked him to. We were going down by the river where there used to be dances every summer; I don't know why they ever quit having them, I believe everyone enjoyed them. The gazebo had a real nice dance floor then. There'd be a live band from the next town over; I remember they wore the nicest straw hats. That's where we were going the first time I wore the dress. But do you think I can find that photograph?"

He didn't move or speak.

She sighed. "Go ahead and put it in the bag."

It turned out to be an hours-long job, putting the fabric into bags. He'd get in a few pieces and she'd say, "Wait!" and come flying back over to his side of the table. She'd examine the red wool, or the yellow printed cotton. "Guess what I made out of this!" she'd say, every time.

"Curtains?" he guessed once, and she said, "Don't be stupid," so he stopped guessing. Something funny happened, though, because after a while, he didn't mind hearing the stories. He was even a little sorry when the bags were all packed.

"Take everything on out to the porch," she said, and she was sad now. "I don't want to look at it anymore."

He brought the bags out and then came back in and stood before her.

"All right, let me get what I owe you," she said. Arthur felt bad taking her money, but his family needed it. His father's business was in the red. Arthur was coming downstairs one night for a glass of milk when he heard his father tell his mother that. His mother asked if maybe he should trade in the horse and wagon for a truck, and he got sore and clammed up until she asked him again. Then he said that all the milk business was going to the goddamn supermarkets, anyway. His mother talked low to him in the same soothing tones she used for her sons when they were upset. "You'll think of something," she said. Arthur knew his dad would be sitting at the kitchen table looking at the floor. His mom would be behind him, her hand on his shoulder, with an odd look of peace on her face. That night, Arthur had crept back up the stairs and asked Frank what *in the red* meant.

"He's losing money; he's not making it in his business," Frank had said. "Seems like everybody's doing better these days but him."

While Mrs. Trentino was off getting her purse, Arthur put his jacket on and looked around the room, whistling.

When Mrs. Trentino returned, she said, "'Peg o' My Heart?'"

"Ma'am?"

"Is that what you were whistling, 'Peg o' My Heart'?"

"Guess I was."

"That's a real nice song. Romantic."

"Yes, ma'am." Arthur liked the part about *Your glances / make my heart say / "How's chances?"*

Mrs. Trentino counted the money into his hands. Dollar and a half.

"Thank you," he said.

"You're welcome. You sure you wouldn't like a cookie?"

He didn't want to refuse her again, and so he said yes, he would, thank you. He ate three awful cookies and drank a glass of milk, and after he was finished he put his dishes in the sink.

"That's a good boy," she said.

"Okay, so . . . see you!" Arthur said.

And naturally he would see her. But he knew that now he would be seeing her in an altogether different way. There she would be, standing fierce on her stoop, but behind her would be a lot of other hers, younger hers, wearing a polka-dotted dress or a red wool suit, or the cotton-print robe she'd had to cut extra-careful to keep whole the wings of the big white birds.

Chapter 4

Before Arthur went to Mrs. Crawford's house, he stopped by Peterson's soda fountain for a scoop of strawberry ice cream. It was a good feeling for a fellow to get paid and then go and spend a bit of his money on something he wanted, just for himself. At first, Arthur ate his ice cream with relish, but by the time his spoon scraped the bottom of the little silver dish, he realized he was missing something. And that was the pleasure of sharing. Of looking over at someone and saying, "Good, huh?" and them saying back, "Sure is!" He'd come to realize people were made for that: sharing, being with one another. It was in him all the time now, this knowledge, and it kind of made his stomach hurt. Frank said it was a biological mandate: people were drawn to others in order to propogate the species. But Arthur suspected it was much more than that. He'd seen that there was an inclination in people to want to give to others in all kinds of ways. If you lost the desire to give, however it happened, you suffered. And you could become bitter and mean. He had thought of Mrs. Trentino as a squinty-eyed old crab, standing on her doorstep with her fists on her hips, yelling at everybody. But today she had told him so much about her life, and Arthur had seen that this gave it back to her, however temporarily. He had been surprisingly entertained by her memories, too. Why, it was like watching a movie, thinking about her dancing with her husband all those years ago! It seemed to Arthur that when you came down to it, every person was like a box of magic: a mysterious vessel full of you-never-knew-what. Old Mrs. Trentino seemed to have said today, *Look at me. I am me.* Arthur did look at her, and he saw her. And both she and Arthur were gentled by that.

Arthur left a tip on the counter and waved goodbye to Eddie Duffy, who was the soda jerk for the day. He was a ruddy-faced, balding man in his mid-fifties, kind and jovial, and best of all someone who understood that when you ordered a scoop you were hoping for a *big* scoop.

Arthur walked toward Mrs. Crawford's house with his hands in his pockets. He passed a couple of squirrels chasing each other around the base of a tree. He stood watching them for a while, thinking about how animals seemed to need companionship, too. The difference was, they weren't shy about it. They didn't *worry* about it. This squirrel currently in pursuit of the other didn't seem to be wondering if he should be chasing it, or if he was doing it right. He hadn't looked at himself in his squirrel mirror before he went out, despairing of his looks. He didn't lie in his bed at night, longing for a particular squirrel and wondering what the future might hold. Or maybe he did. It amused Arthur, at any rate, to think that a squirrel might do that, too. Whoever said misery loves company was right.

Mrs. Crawford had forty different varieties of roses. But here was Arthur out in her garden, digging holes for more. Everybody thought it was crazy how much time and attention Mrs. Crawford put into her rose garden, including Arthur. But Mrs. Crawford had told him a few interesting things about those flowers. For one thing, roses were really old; they'd been found in fossils from millions of years ago. Also, yellow roses were for friendship, but red roses were for love. And if you gave someone seven red roses, that meant the strongest love of all. Not a dozen; seven. Maybe someday he'd give Nola seven roses, and she'd count them and say, "Why seven?" and he'd tell her. By then, he'd know how to tell her.

The most interesting thing Mrs. Crawford told Arthur about roses, though, was that you could eat them. That's what she said. He couldn't quite imagine how you would do that.

Arthur liked working for Mrs. Crawford, even if he was just digging holes. She had thick blond hair that she pulled back with combs. She painted her nails red. She had clear blue eyes that looked like they were in on the joke. When you were around her, you felt like she thought you were just swell; Arthur thought she had a way of making people feel like they were better than they probably were.

Sometimes the two of them worked in the garden together, and on hot days she wore shorts and a halter top. Every boy in town had a crush on her, but of course that was like standing at a store window, wishing for the most expensive thing. Not one of the boys thought seriously that they would ever have a chance to so much as kiss her hand. But women like Mrs. Crawford were made for dreaming about, same as the calendar girls some dads kept in basement workrooms.

Just before Arthur went home from helping her, Mrs. Crawford would always cut a bunch of roses for him to give to his mother, who would set them out on the dining room table in a cut-crystal vase that had been *her* mother's. She would stop to admire those flowers every day, probably a few times a day. He saw her once, standing before them, her dust rag in her hand, her apron sagging at the neck. He wondered if when she looked at the flowers it felt like she were somewhere else. Someplace grand, like the lobby of the Palmer House Hotel, where there were murals and gold candelabras on the high ceiling. His mother had a faded postcard of that place stuck into her mirror.

Years ago, Arthur's mother had told him about how she'd been taken there by some fellow she dated before she got married. She'd been washing the supper dishes, and Arthur had been drying. "It was a Saturday morning, a

beautiful spring day," his mother had said. "We took the
train clear to Chicago and back, just because I'd told him I
wanted to see the lobby at the Palmer House Hotel." It was
a long trip, she'd told Arthur, but that was all part of the
adventure: the train, the people on it, the changing views
she saw out those big windows. She didn't get to spend
much time in the lobby, but she got to see it. "That ceiling!" she'd said. "And the fancy people there! And the flowers everywhere!" She'd rinsed out a glass and handed it to
him, and it seemed to him that she'd grown suddenly sad.

"Why don't you go and see it again?" Arthur had
asked, and she'd said she'd see it again someday.

"How old were you when you did that?" Arthur asked,
always a point of interest for him when his parents had
done certain things in their lives.

"I had just turned seventeen," his mother said.

"Did your parents know you went?"

"I didn't tell them."

"So they didn't know."

"Well . . . No, they didn't. They would have worried,
you see."

"But nothing happened."

"No, but they would have worried."

"Who *was* that guy who took you there?" Arthur
asked.

His mother smiled and shook her head a little, like she
wouldn't say. But then a second later, she slid her eyes over
to Arthur and said quietly, "Julian was his name."

"Holy moly. He must have been crazy for you. It had to
have set him back some, buying those tickets."

"He did like me an awful lot."

"What happened to *him*?" Arthur asked, and his mother got all brisk and businesslike to say he'd married someone else. Then he'd moved away.

"Where'd he go?" Arthur had asked, and she'd pointed to the dish rack and said, "Keep up, Arthur."

They did the dishes together every night, something Arthur enjoyed, because his mother often got dreamy with her hands in the warm soapy water, and she told him things she might not otherwise.

That night, up in their bedroom, Arthur had shared with Frank the story about Julian. Arthur worried a little about betraying what felt like his mother's confidence, but he had to tell his brother.

The story had given Frank, who was then thirteen, an idea. He had a friend whose parents had a typewriter, and the next morning, Frank and Arthur went over to his house so Frank could type a letter to their mother that she was supposed to think was from Julian. It said that his wife had died and he had never forgotten their mother, who had been his one true love, and that he was sorrier than he could say that he hadn't married her. *I am loath to understand why,* Frank had written, and then he'd had to explain to Arthur what the word *loath* meant. "Julian" wanted their mother to leave her husband and marry him; would she consider that? He'd adopt any children she might have (that had been Arthur's idea, to put in something about him and Frank) and they could all live together in his house in Milwaukee; he had a big mansion by the lake. Frank let Arthur be the one to sign the letter, and they went home and put it in the mailbox.

Their mother hadn't fallen for it for one second, of course. For one thing, the letter had no stamp. The return address had no surname, and the street they made up for Julian to live on was Millionaire's Lane. Their mother had come to their room that afternoon after the mail had been delivered; Arthur and Frank were up there putting together a model plane, and the scent of the glue was thick in the air.

She'd leaned against the doorjamb and pulled the letter out of her apron pocket. She held it up, saying nothing. Frank and Arthur were trying not to smile.

"Hi, Ma," Frank said.

"Do you need us?" Arthur asked.

Their mother had ripped the letter in half, then ripped it again. She shoved the pieces back in her apron pocket, hard. "Don't you ever do anything like this again," she said, and her voice was low and flat. She'd started to walk out of the room but then she spun around. "Do you think this is funny?"

They'd become unmoving, their heads down.

She walked over to stand right beside them. "Do you think this is *funny*, I asked you."

In a low and barely audible voice, Frank said, "We just wanted to make you feel good, like Julian still—"

Their mother slammed her hand on the table, and one of the airplane parts they'd just glued on fell off. They'd kept looking down, ashamed, but then Arthur ventured to look up and there were tears in his mother's eyes and they spilled over. And they were tiny little tears; he'd been struck by that, how tiny they were. She'd wiped them away with a fury he'd not seen in her before, and went downstairs.

"Fix that," Frank had said, pointing to the part that had fallen off the model. While Arthur did, Frank had gone to stand at the window, where he'd pressed his forehead against the glass and closed his eyes. Then he'd muttered an expletive Arthur could not say, not then or ever in his life.

And so, years later, Arthur brought his mother roses at every opportunity, his version of the Palmer House lobby, a memory held in petals.

When Arthur had begun working for Mrs. Crawford, he'd asked his mother why she didn't try planting a few rosebushes of her own. She'd said she was too busy to fuss with them. Arthur guessed maybe she was. He guessed he wasn't aware of all she did. Home was a place where everyone spun in their own orbits. Except that every night, up in their room, for as long as he could remember, Frank and Arthur had lain in the dark and talked. No topic was off-limits, even when Arthur was worried for so long that a certain part of his anatomy had something wrong with it, veering off to the left the way it did. When he finally told his brother about it, Frank said that was completely normal. Arthur was wide-eyed with relief.

There was always something they needed to discuss. Arthur relied upon it. There was the sun coming up and the sun going down, and there was Frank and Arthur whispering to each other every night in the dark. In this way, they spun out a line that Arthur believed would tie them together forever.

Chapter 5

ON MONDAY, AFTER school, Arthur was alone in his bedroom, unable to concentrate on his homework. He was beset by a particular kind of restlessness, and Frank, who was at baseball practice, wasn't there to talk to. A thunderstorm was predicted for later that afternoon, and Arthur decided to take a walk while he could.

"Don't be gone long," his mother said. "Look at that sky."

"I know," Arthur told her. He'd seen the dark and roiling clouds from the window.

"Take your jacket," his mother said, and Arthur didn't bother to say it was warm out. He put on his jacket.

He was half a block away when he saw lightning and heard a low rumble of thunder. Still, he kept on. If he had to run home, he'd run home.

He was nearing Main Street when the rain started falling. He pulled up his jacket collar and started to turn back but then caught sight of a familiar figure, hunched over a bag of groceries. "Nola!" he called, and he began walking quickly toward her.

She looked up and smiled. "Arthur! Look at us, out here in Armageddon!"

"I hardly think it's that," Arthur said. And then, as drops began falling faster, he said, "Want me to take that bag for you?"

"Well, if you'd hold it for a second, I'd appreciate it. I've got a rain bonnet in my purse."

Arthur took the bag and snuck a look at what was in there. He wanted to know everything about Nola. At the top of the bag were celery, potatoes, and a box of Argo cornstarch. Nothing exactly revealing, but it was hers.

She finished tying on her rain bonnet, then took the bag from him. "Thanks!" she said. The rain was falling harder, and she had to talk loudly to be heard. "We'd better get going!"

"Want me to carry your bag home for you?"

"What?" She blinked her eyes against the rain.

He repeated his question, and she reached out to touch his cheek. "Oh, Arthur, you're too sweet."

He held out his arms to take the bag, but she pulled it closer to herself. The paper was beginning to sag with the wetness; it wouldn't hold much longer. "I'm going to run home," she said. "You should, too." Her rain bonnet slipped off her head and she yanked it back up, which did a pretty good job of messing up her hair: it stood erect like a rooster's comb.

"I must look a fright," she said.

"You look beautiful," he said, and she did: her face flushed with color, her eyes bright.

She laughed. "See you in school tomorrow," she said. She began to run, but turned around long enough to shout, "Bye, Arthur!"

Now he was getting thoroughly drenched, but he stood watching her go. Only when she had disappeared around the corner did he start for home himself.

When Arthur came into the bedroom after washing up, he found Frank lying in bed, reading a book by one of his favorite writers, John Steinbeck. *The Grapes of Wrath*, it was called, which Arthur found to be a peculiar title.

Arthur sat at his desk. "I thought you finished that book," he said.

Frank lay the book down on the bed and rubbed at one of his eyes. "I'm reading it again. Not for the story this time, but for the technique."

"What do you mean?"

"Well, suppose you wanted to be a mechanic. You'd bring your car in for them to fix, but then you would want to watch to see how they did it."

"You want to be a mechanic?" Arthur asked.

"No. I want to be a writer." He looked sharply at his brother. "Don't tell anybody."

Arthur shrugged. "Okay."

"I mean it, Arthur."

"It's a secret?"

"Well, it's . . . Yeah. It's kind of a secret. If you tell someone you want to be a writer, they start asking you all kinds of questions. Questions I don't have the answers to yet. Questions I don't want to think about because it might be like a jinx or something. And also, if you say you're a writer, people want to see something you wrote. And I'm not ready to show anybody anything. Nobody but—"

"Miss Anker."

"Right."

"You showed her a story you wrote, right?"

"I showed her a story I'm working on. It's not done. It might never be done. I'm just working on it."

"What's it about?"

Frank sighed. "I can't really say, you know? It's about a lot of stuff. Like if I tell you what it's *about,* it won't say *all* that it's about."

"But can't you just say . . . you know, 'It's a story about a cat that lives under the porch'?"

"That would be the story?" Frank asked.

"Okay, it would be about a cat that lives under a porch and one day he saves his owner's life."

"How's he do *that*?"

"*I* don't know!" Arthur said. "I'm not a writer!"

"Well, if you *were* a writer and you wrote a story about a cat who saved his owner's life, it would be about that life being saved, but it would be about *more* than that. It would *suggest* more than that."

Frank picked up the book and turned to a page he had marked. "Let me read you something, okay?"

Arthur didn't mean to say it aloud, but it slipped out: "Is it long?"

Frank just looked at him. If it were up to him, Arthur believed Frank would read to him all day long. But Arthur had homework to do tonight, including math, which was slow torture. Plus useless.

"I like when you read to me, but . . ." Arthur held up his algebra book.

"I'll help you with your algebra. Cripes, it's only seven-thirty."

"I have civics, too," Arthur said.

"All right, I'll help you get your algebra done. But I want you to try to do it yourself first. Go ahead."

Arthur pulled his chair up close to his desk and sat straight and still, staring at the first problem in his book. He blinked, looked up at the ceiling, then stared at the problem some more. He wrote down a few figures, then erased them. Wrote down some different ones, erased them. He contemplated the eraser at the end of his pencil. Whoever invented erasers must have known all about algebra. He wondered who *did* invent erasers. That would be interesting to find out. He held his pencil up closer to his eyes, examining the eraser. Rubber came from trees, and—

"Arthur!" Frank said. "You're not even trying!"

"I *am,*" Arthur said.

Frank sighed. He got up and came to stand by Arthur's desk, his hands on his hips like a football player. "Show me the problem," he said. Then, "Man alive! What'd you put on yourself?"

"Aftershave," Arthur told Frank, not looking at him. He'd bought some at the drugstore that afternoon.

"You ever heard the term 'whorehouse'?"

Arthur felt himself flushing. "Yes."

"Well, that's what you smell like."

"Are you going to help me with my homework or not?"

"So what's the deal, Arthur, you got a girlfriend?"

"Matter of fact, I do."

"What's her name?"

"Name's Nola Corrine McCollum."

Frank whistled a dropping-bomb sound. "Nola? That sophomore? She won't give you the time of day. The *senior* boys are all dying for her. Aim lower."

Arthur looked up at him. "For your information, she gave me her telephone number." Arthur thought again about the way she'd said "See you in school tomorrow" after they'd finished talking in the rain, like maybe she was really looking forward to it. Maybe after she got home she'd sat at her own desk thinking, *Hmmm. Arthur Moses.* Maybe she'd doodled his name.

Frank interrupted his reverie. "You're talking about that one with the long black hair, right? And real big blue eyes?"

"Yes." The long black hair, those blue eyes a guy felt he might fall right into. The sweet blush of pink in her cheeks, a little mole above her lip you'd notice only if you were close to her. The bobby socks turned down just so. The delicate ankles that reminded Arthur of Thoroughbred horses, which of course he would never tell her, in case she took his meaning wrong.

"You got her *number*?" Frank said. "Really?"

Arthur pulled the slip of paper from his desk drawer and waved it around.

Frank started to grab it, and Arthur snatched it back.

Frank sat on the edge of Arthur's desk and crossed his arms. "Well, well, well. So did you call her? What'd you two talk about?"

"Are you going to help me with my algebra or not?" Arthur asked. If only he had a wristwatch, he could look at it importantly now. He didn't want to admit he hadn't called Nola.

"All right, all right," Frank said. "Show me the problem."

Later, after they got into their beds and turned out the lights, Frank asked, "So how'd this happen, you and Nola?"

Arthur looked over at him, indistinct in the dark. "You know how you said you can't answer questions about writing? Well, I can't answer questions about her. Not yet."

"I respect that."

Arthur raised himself up on one elbow. "But you want a good story? Get a load of what happened when I went to Mrs. Trentino's house."

Arthur told Frank about the way Mrs. Trentino wanted to talk about all those pieces of fabric; how at first it had really annoyed him, but then he'd liked it. He said, "I guess I came to like her, 'cause of what she told me about all those things she made, and the summer dances and all. Especially her asking her husband, 'Would you take a picture of how I look?' Almost like she knew there'd come a day when she might forget, and she didn't want to. But she lost that dress and she lost her husband and then she lost the photograph, too. And now she was losing the cloth she'd made it out of. I don't know. I feel sorry for her. When people lose so much, what do they do?"

"I guess they find other things."

"But what can you find good when you're so *old*?"

Arthur could see the white of Frank's teeth when he smiled. "*That* would make a story. Imagine if—"

They stopped talking then; they could hear a heavy tread on the stairs leading up to their room.

Their father pushed the door open. The stairway light behind him made him look bigger than he was.

"Frank."

"Yes, sir?"

"Have you been spending time down by the tracks?"

"The tracks?"

"Yeah. The tracks."

"Have I been spending *time* there?"

"Have you got a hearing problem?"

"No, sir, I don't believe so."

"Answer the question, then."

"No, I haven't been spending time at the tracks."

"Well, that's interesting. Because Don Taylor just

called and he told me somebody he knows saw you hanging around with the lowlifes who congregate there."

"I wouldn't say that."

"You wouldn't say that, huh? What would you say, then?"

"What do you mean, 'lowlifes,' Pop?" Arthur asked. He was trying to help Frank. "What does that mean, 'lowlifes'?"

His father jerked his head toward Arthur. "Stay out of this." He moved closer to Frank's bed and stood over him, swaying a little.

"I don't hang around down there," Frank said. "It wasn't me Don saw."

"Mr. Taylor."

"It wasn't me Mr. Taylor saw."

"It better not have been. Those people down there are nothing but trash, not worth spitting on."

"Yeah, a real bad lot, huh?" Frank said, and Arthur could hear the grin behind his words.

So could their father, he imagined. But he just said, "Do not let me hear about you being there again. Those people will rob you blind, Frank. They'll rough you up just for something to do. They're no good. There's something wrong with every one of them."

"Yes, sir."

Their father stood there a bit longer, and then he told Frank, "I'm trying to help you, son."

"I know it, Pop."

"There was a bad thing happened down there the other

day. Somebody trying to cross the tracks got the living daylights beat out of them. They jumped him. Broad daylight."

"Is that right?"

"That's right."

"Okay."

"Are we straight?"

"Yeah, we're straight."

Their father slapped his newspaper against his leg a few times, then walked out, closing the door behind him.

After a few minutes, Frank whispered, "Arthur."

"Yeah?"

"You know what's wrong with the people down at the tracks?"

Arthur didn't say anything.

"They've had some bad luck is all. They've had some hard things happen to them that broke them a little. It could happen to anyone. But they're not bad people. I'll show you. You want to come down there with me sometime? I'll introduce you to that fortune teller. She can tell you things about Nola."

"In private?"

"Of course. That's the only way she'll do it. She'll take you into a boxcar and do a reading for you. You'll have to give her a little something, two bits, or maybe fifty cents."

"Fifty cents!"

"You won't regret it. You want to do it or not?"

"Okay," Arthur said. "But what if the boxcar starts moving?"

"Then you jump off. Dingbat."

Quiet, and then Frank said, "They're really not bad people. I cut across the tracks all the time to go to Mary's house. Not one of them has ever been threatening in any way."

" 'Mary,' huh?" Arthur couldn't imagine calling Miss Anker by her first name. It seemed odd to realize that teachers *came* with first names.

"Mary Margaret," Frank said. "I call her Mags sometimes."

Well, this whole thing was out of Arthur's hands. He rolled over onto his side, away from Frank, who seemed like he was becoming less and less his brother every day. He was moving somewhere else.

"Know how we're going to have dinner every night after we're married?" Frank asked.

"How?" Oh, Arthur was miserable. He was breathing into a little pocket of sheet he had pulled up over his nose.

"By candlelight. No reason we can't. We're going to eat by candlelight and have music playing on the radio in the background. She likes music an awful lot. She can play piano."

Arthur supposed she'd teach Frank to play. He supposed they'd be sitting on the bench together, smiling, and here he would be. He and Mrs. Trentino, mourning their losses. Some people got everything they wanted, just like that. Others had to wait and wait and maybe it would come and maybe it wouldn't.

"Can I tell you something, Arthur? Mary's going to

help me become a writer. I mean it. A real writer, and then once I start getting my books published, she can quit working and I'll support her. She's got a nice house and she keeps it up fine, but I'll get her something even better. I'll buy her everything she wants. Soon as I graduate, we're going to move to New York City."

Arthur turned over. "You are?"

"Yeah! Wouldn't you, if you could?"

"No! I want to live here."

"All your *life*?"

Now Arthur was a little ashamed, but he said, "I guess I like it here more than you do." He thought of things he might say to Frank about why he loved Mason. How the bakery ladies all knew his name. How old Pots Adams sat out on his front porch step every morning in his battered leather slippers and stretched-out suspenders, waving to the little kids on their way to school. In the afternoon, when they were on their way home, he'd be out there again, shouting "How went the battle?" just to see them laugh. Arthur loved Mason's slow-running river, the deep green of the park, the way the wooden pews of the church practically glowed when the light was right. He liked how Mr. Spurlock always waited to buy his Christmas tree until the last minute so he could get a good deal, and then his wife made him keep it on the porch for the way it dropped its needles like crazy, so there was a fully deco-rated Christmas tree right out in the open for all the pass-ersby to enjoy. Why, you could never get *lost* in Mason, and that meant something to Arthur. But you couldn't always persuade people to your point of view, no matter what you said. You had to let them make up their own minds. He hoped Nola liked Mason. He hoped she'd want to live here forever, as he did. He hoped she'd want to live with *him*. Oh, what a feeling, imagining coming into a kitchen that they shared. Saying "Good morning" to her every day. Saying "Good night"!

Frank had crossed his arms behind his head and was staring up at the ceiling. Arthur could make out the line of his arm muscles. Arthur figured he got them from working at the grocery store. It didn't seem to matter how much digging in the garden Arthur did, he didn't have muscles like that. He wondered if such things mattered to Nola. Not *every* girl cared if you were a he-man.

Frank said, "You'll come for a visit after we move, Mary and I. You'll see how wonderful New York is and then you'll want to move there, too."

"But you haven't even been there!" Arthur said. "You've only seen it in the movies."

"And that's enough for me. You know, sometimes you're not born in the place you're meant to be. You've got to figure it out, take the clues that life offers you, and then you've got to gin up the courage to act. Nobody's going to live your life for you."

Arthur thought about this. He wondered if maybe Nola had been giving him clues for a while that he just hadn't seen, and, if so, how he should act on them. He wasn't the type to swoop Nola up and carry her down the hall like he'd seen a wrestler at school, Tommy Nolan, do with his girlfriend, Poodles O'Hara. That wasn't her real name, she just got called Poodles because of her curly hair. But Tommy Nolan scooped her up and she laughed and screamed all the way down the hall, pretend-beating on his shoulders. Arthur couldn't do anything like that. If he tried to carry a girl, he'd probably drop her. And there she'd be, pulling her skirt down all embarrassed and probably yelling at him. He wasn't the type who could write Nola a letter that would be any good, either.

Well, she'd have to come around in her own time. She'd have to come to love him for his pure self. It would take some time. But he thought they'd begun *some*thing. Years from now, maybe they'd laugh about the day when Nola asked about Frank, when it was Arthur who loved her so.

Then Frank said something that made him think his brother was reading his mind. "Maybe you'll marry Nola. And then the two of you can move to New York, too."

Arthur snorted. "Yeah, sure." He was trying to be jokey and nonchalant though he was anything but. It came to him that this was what true love was: you weren't happy; you were miserable, lying in bed with your guts aching, hope hanging above you like a balloon with a string you couldn't quite reach.

Frank said, "You know, Arthur, the thing about girls is you can't give them too much right away. You've got to give them tastes, and then they get intrigued and want to come back for more."

"I don't know what I could give Nola McCollum a taste of."

"She must have some interest in you! She gave you her phone number!"

"Yes, but it was . . . It was for a question she had," Arthur said.

"About what?"

About what. "Something she wanted me to look up for her in my tree book. She's doing a report on white oaks."

Arthur didn't feel too bad fibbing to Frank. His brother was busy. In a way, Arthur was doing him a favor.

Frank turned on his bedside light. Arthur squinted and held his arm over his eyes. "What are you doing?" he whispered.

"I'm getting you something." Frank went over to the bookcase he'd made in shop class, a real nice little pine one with dovetail joints. He'd made it to keep all the books he brought home from the library or bought for cheap at church basement fundraisers. He'd nearly filled the case. He crouched in front of it, scanning the titles, and then he pulled one out and handed it to Arthur.

Arthur looked at the gently deteriorating spine. "*Riders of the Purple Sage?*"

"Yup. Also known as 'Zane Grey's Guide to Women.'" He climbed back in bed and turned out his light again.

"This guy's name is *Zane*?"

"It's a great name, isn't it? And his hero is a gunslinger named Lassiter. I know you like all your nature books, but you can learn other things from books, too. Read that one and see how things go with Lassiter and Jane. He knows all the right moves."

Arthur thought he was going to like this book. Also, he was beginning to sympathize with men who sat in the barbershop talking about how hard it was to figure out women.

"See," Frank said, "the thing about girls is you want to be honest, but you need to hold back sometimes, too. Give a little, hold back a little. You've got to be patient while you're reeling them in. But once you have them, why, then you give them everything. That's what I did with Mary, and now I've got her. I can't even tell you how deep this love is. It's not because she's so pretty, either. It's because our insides match. I knew it the moment I saw her. It can happen like that."

"I'm real glad for you, Frank."

"Your turn will come."

"I know," Arthur said, but at present he sure didn't see quite how. The only thing he could see for sure was that love had made a liar out of him, just as it had Frank. Here, they were equal.

Chapter 6

IT WASN'T OFTEN that Arthur woke up ahead of the time he needed to for school, but this morning he did. Fully half an hour before he had to leave the house, he was ready to go. It felt to him like something was going to *happen* today; he was jumpy in the glad way.

"I'm going outside to wait for Frank," he told his mother, and he went to sit on the front steps, where he watched the birds flitting in and out of the oak trees in front of his house. Some of them were so pretty, colored red or yellow or blue; he thought they looked like living jewels. And they were such skillful flyers: their quick lift-offs and landings, the way they moved their tail feathers to change direction. Frank had told him birds were perfect for flying because of their hollow bones, and because their shape minimized aerodynamic drag. Sometimes when Arthur was watching a bird fly, he'd see an airplane high above it. *No contest,* he always thought.

Birds were entertaining, too. If you paid attention, you could see individual personalities: the ones who would fly away at the tiniest movement, the ones who would almost let you reach out and pet them. Greedy eaters, dainty ones. Birds who reveled in taking baths in puddles, others who were content to stand nearby and watch. Some birds would call back to you when you whistled, and you could spend half a day trading calls with that jukebox of avians, the mockingbird. So much to see in nature, just in the birds alone. Add in the flowers and the trees and the ever-changing sky, and you had paradise. That was what Arthur liked best about nature, the *givingness* of it.

Just now, there was some unusual activity going on between two robins. It looked like they were having a fight. One would settle on a branch; the other would fly up and settle right next to it. The first robin would move to another branch; the other bird would follow. Finally, the first bird lit out across the street, flying fast, but the other bird was right behind.

Yup, a fight, unless . . . *Oh,* Arthur thought suddenly. *Spring. Babies. Courtship.*

Arthur saw why he had awakened early. This was the day he needed to make a bolder move toward Nola. He'd been ready before he knew he was ready.

After school, Arthur raced out of the building and waited until he saw Nola come out, walking with a group of girls. They were all talking and laughing, twirling around and such. It made him hesitant to butt in, but he cried out, "Hey, Nola!"

She stopped walking and looked over at him.

"Hi, Arthur!" she said.

All the other girls had stopped walking and now they looked at him, too. He held up a hand and waved to the girls. Wrong move; they snuck smiley little glances at one other.

Well, what would Zane Grey do? "I want to talk to you for a minute," Arthur said. Then, boldly, he added, "Privately."

"Go on without me," Nola told her friends. "I'll catch up."

Arthur straightened his back to stand taller as she walked over to him. She was wearing a red sweater set and a plaid pleated skirt. The white on her saddle shoes was unscuffed. She did not have a comb stuck in her socks like the tough girls did. He began rehearsing in his head: *Nola, we need to get something straight.* Here, he would step closer and look right into her eyes. *I want to tell you something.*

"Did you do it?" Nola asked.

He was confused. "Do what?"

She looked around as though they were being spied on. "Did you give my *number* to *Frank*?" Her breath smelled good, like clove gum. "I've been dying to hear what happened," she said.

Well, this was not what he was expecting. Here he'd been having all these exuberant thoughts, while she had apparently been thinking another way entirely.

"You *did* give it to him, didn't you?" Nola asked.

"You asked me to, right?"

He hadn't lied. Not yet. And now he was going to make his move. He cleared his throat, raised his eyebrows. "So anyway, I was wondering—"

"What did he say?" Nola asked.

"What did he *say*? He didn't say anything, really. He just looked at it. And then he . . . you know, put it in his desk drawer."

"He didn't say *any*thing?"

"Well, he said your name. He said, 'Hmm. Nola McCollum.'"

"But how did he *look* saying it?"

Arthur thought it must be time to do a little of that holding back Frank had told him about.

"I'll tell you what. Let's go over to Peterson's and I'll buy you a soda. We can talk there."

She looked closely at him. She was onto him, Arthur thought, and he was starting to sweat. Just then, a car pulled over to the curb and honked its horn. Nola looked over, laughed and waved. It was a bunch of kids, shouting at her to *Get in, get in!* They were doing a pile-on; they already had a lot of kids in there. But Nola shook her head no, and the car drove off.

"All right, come on, then," Nola said, and she looped her arm through his.

"Carry your books?" he asked, and his voice cracked.

But she just said, "Sure, thanks," like she didn't even notice. And then they were walking together, Nola McCollum and Arthur Moses.

"I have to be home by five," Nola said, and Arthur said, "I'll have you home by four fifty-nine," in a blessedly lower voice, and with a kind of authority that surprised him.

She looked over at him. "You know what? I never noticed this before, but you're kinda cute."

See? You took one step in a certain direction, and just like that, you were off. Arthur was ebullient now. "You're not so bad yourself," he said, and snuck a look over at her. She was smiling, so he guessed it was an okay thing to say.

They ordered root-beer floats, and Arthur saw a couple at the end of the counter who were sharing one drink with two straws, their foreheads touching. *Someday,* he thought.

"Would you care for anything else?" he asked Nola when their floats were delivered.

"No, thanks, this is great."

Good thing. He barely had any money left.

Nola took a sip of her drink and said, "Well?"

He knew what she meant. He'd told her they'd discuss Frank more.

Arthur shrugged. "So, as I said, he just said your name."

"Like he was pleased?" She seemed nervous; her voice was small.

"Well, of course he was pleased. Who wouldn't be?"

Nola didn't look convinced.

The bell on the door tinkled, and Doreen Majors came in with Ducks Tilton. Ducks was wearing a letter jacket that made him look twice the size he was, and he had his chest all stuck out. Doreen's eyes were glowy.

"*Nola!*" Doreen said, as if they hadn't seen each other in a hundred years.

"Hi, Doreen."

"Well, I am fit to be tied!"

"Oh?"

Arthur raised his chin at Ducks, who came over and said, "How's it going, Moses?"

"Not bad." Arthur was thrilled Ducks had called him by his last name. That was because of Nola. You just sat with her and right away you started being treated like a popular person.

Ducks started talking about the last basketball game, but Arthur was mostly listening to Nola and Doreen. Doreen said that Suzie Templeton had heard about the slumber party Doreen was having Saturday night, and the last thing she wanted was for *Suzie Templeton* to think she'd get an invitation to be with *them.*

"Hmmm," Nola said.

"I mean, can you imagine? I had to think fast and say it was *next* Saturday. Won't that be funny? Her showing up on the wrong day? Oh, I'll apologize and all. 'So *sorry*! I can't believe I *did* that! We were all *wondering* where you were!'"

"Where's Frank been?" Ducks asked Arthur. "He quit coming to practice."

Nola had been listening to Doreen talking about the wild hairdo contest they were going to have at the slumber party. But when she heard Frank's name, she turned to listen to Arthur and Ducks.

"Frank's been real busy at work," Arthur said.

"But is he coming back to the team?"

"I don't think so. You'd have to ask him."

"Well, he's your *brother,* Moses. You don't talk?"

"Not really," Arthur said.

"Ducks!" some guy called from a booth against the wall, and Ducks grabbed Doreen's arm.

"Come on," he said, and Doreen went right along, grinning like a fool.

"She's mean," Arthur said to Nola. "I'm sorry to say that about your friend. But she's mean."

"I'm not going to her party anymore," Nola said, and she stared down into her lap.

"You're nothing like her," Arthur said.

Nola looked at him. "You don't know me!"

"I know that much," Arthur said. "And since you'll now be free on Saturday night, maybe you'd like to go somewhere with me." His stomach clenched.

"Where?"

"The movies? Seven o'clock show?"

She stared at him, her head tilted. It seemed to Arthur that a few days passed. But finally she said, "All right, Arthur. I'd like that."

Arthur exhaled slowly. Done. A date with Nola McCollum on Saturday night, the big one.

When Arthur walked Nola home, she was quiet for a while. Then she said, "Can I ask you one more thing about Frank?"

"Sure," Arthur said, and stopped himself from sighing.

"Do you think it's stupid for me to be interested in him?"

Arthur thought about what to say. Finally, he said, "I don't think it's stupid. He's a pretty great guy."

Nola nodded. "He is. But sometimes I think I say I want something just because . . ."

"Because what?" Arthur asked.

"Never mind."

"What were you going to say?" he asked, but now they were in front of her house.

She turned to him and now she was smiling. "Thanks for everything, Arthur. I'm really glad we . . . Well, I'm glad we're getting to know each other a little more."

"Me, too."

She took her books, ran up her front-porch steps, and turned around. "We'll have fun on Saturday. See you at school tomorrow!"

Arthur had quite the giddy-up in his step when he walked home. He couldn't wait to tell Frank about the progress he'd made. Advance to Boardwalk. He couldn't help it; he started whistling.

Chapter 7

A RTHUR'S FATHER HAD been let go, and he seemed to have no idea what to do next. He sat glowering at dinner until finally Frank said, "Seems like a lot of people are hiring, Pop."

"Oh, they are, are they?"

"Lot of jobs in what they call postwar industry."

"Such as?"

"Well, read the want ads!"

Their father stopped eating, his fork midair.

"I just mean there's all kinds of things," Frank said, his voice more subdued. "Construction. Mail carrier."

"You think I can do that with my back?"

"Maybe an office job, then. Whitey McPherson's dad just got an office job selling insurance. He likes it fine, and he said it pays good."

"Muriel Anderson's husband got a job selling cars," their mother said, but their father ignored her and kept his eyes on Frank.

"Let me ask you something. Did I ask your advice?"

"No, sir."

"Eugene," Arthur's mother said softly.

His father held up his hand. "No. I want to know what makes him think it's so easy for a guy like me to just go out and find another job. I didn't graduate high school like he's going to. So why don't you tell me, Frank, why you think it's so easy?"

Frank was staring at his plate. But then he looked up, and any fear he might have had seemed to be gone.

"Honestly, Pop? Can I tell you something? I think it's your attitude more than your skills holding you back. Alls you need to do is—"

Their father stood up fast, his napkin in his hand.

"Eugene," Arthur's mother said, and now her voice was firm. A warning.

His father looked over at her, threw down his napkin, and then left the house, slamming the kitchen door behind him. From the window they could see him walking quickly down the sidewalk, his head down, his fists jammed into his pockets.

Arthur's mother stood and removed her husband's plate from the table with empty-eyed efficiency. "Finish your dinner," she told her sons. Then, more softly, "There's apple pie."

Arthur had sat at the kitchen table, watching her make that pie. When she'd peeled the apples, she'd cut carefully around the bad spots. When she'd added cold water to the crust and mixed it in, she'd told him, "You always think it's not going to come together, but then it always does."

"I don't see how you do that," Arthur had said admiringly.

She'd smiled over at him. "Do you want me to teach you how to make an apple pie, Arthur?"

"Boys don't cook!"

"Well, of course they do! I had a young man make me dinner once. He had me over to his place; it was just a room in a boardinghouse, but he had me over for spaghetti and meatballs that he'd made on a hotplate. He had a little table all laid out with a white cloth and a candle, and he had wildflowers in a milk bottle. *And* he sang me a song in Italian before we ate."

"He was Italian?"

"He was."

"And he *sang* to you?"

"Seemed like we were always doing crazy things, back then. We were so young."

"Who was *that* guy?"

"It was a long time ago. Go and do your homework."

By the time Arthur and Frank went upstairs for bed, their dad still hadn't come home. He'd done it before, taken off like that, in one of his moods. He'd be back, but there was no predicting what he'd be like when he returned.

"You awake?" Frank asked Arthur.

"Yeah."

"I think we should stay up until he gets back."

"Okay."

"You got anything you want to talk about?"

Arthur remembered suddenly that he did. Holy smokes, of course he did!

"Well, for one thing, I bought Nola McCollum a root-beer float today."

"Seriously?"

"Yup."

"She went with you? Willingly?"

"Very funny. Yes, she did. And not only that, I'm taking her to the movies on Saturday night." After which he would have no money left, but that was what jobs were for: earning money. He wondered now, though, if he'd have to start giving more to the family and keep less for himself.

"That's big, Arthur. You could try to kiss her after you walk her home."

"On the *first date*?"

"It can be done. You need to judge the mood. Like, if she leans against your shoulder in the movie, it can be done. If she lingers on the porch after you walk her home, if she stands there like she's waiting for something. And then, remember, *leave her wanting more*."

Arthur didn't want to ask any more questions. He didn't want to rely on Frank for *every*thing. But thus far his brother's advice had done a lot of good. So, "How do I leave her wanting more?" he asked.

"Well," Frank said, "kiss her only once, for one thing. Even if she gets kind of dreamy-eyed, even if she leans in toward you afterward, don't kiss her twice. And when you do kiss her that first and only time, be really gentle. You could put your hands on the sides of her face, push your fingers up into her hair a little. They like that. And after the kiss, pull away slowly and look into her eyes."

Arthur was trying to imagine doing this when he heard the kitchen door open downstairs, then close.

"He's home," Frank whispered.

"I'll bet he feels bad," Arthur whispered back.

"He won't. He'll feel like it's all my fault. There's some guys just have a chip on their shoulder. They feel like the world is against them, like they never get a fair shake. They don't realize that a lot of the time, luck is something you make for yourself."

Arthur thought it was true. Look at him and Nola today. It was lucky that he got to be with her, but he realized now that he'd made that luck for himself.

"It's sad, really," Frank said. "If he'd just—"

He stopped talking. Here came their father's uneven tread, coming up the stairs to the second floor. There was the sound of a stumble, followed by a muffled curse. Their parents' bedroom door opened, then closed. The boys could hear their father talking to their mother, but they couldn't make out what he was saying.

"What does she *see* in him?" Arthur whispered.

"Beats me," Frank said. "But one thing I've learned about love and people being together is that you just can't predict. You can have a really attractive person fall hard for someone who isn't much of anything. Take Ma and Pop. She's just great, gentle and pretty and kind. She's got a good sense of humor, and she's a good conversationalist. He's not like that at all. Silent type. Brooding. Quick to hold a grudge. But she must get *something* out of him that we just can't see. For some reason, she felt that he was the one for her."

"Maybe it's that some people like taking care of hurt people," Arthur said. "Way I see Pop, he's hurt; and Ma gets something out of trying to fix him. Remember how we had that bird one time, that had flown into the window, and we nursed him back until he could fly away? Maybe she sees Pop that way."

Frank was quiet for a while. Then he said, "Well, he didn't have it easy coming up, that's for sure. But like I was trying to tell him at dinner, he mostly has an attitude problem. He doesn't try. He seems to always gravitate toward the negative side of things. You watch a baseball game with him and you say something about how the pitcher's having a really good day and he'll say, 'Yeah, well, let's just see how long *that* lasts.'"

"But he *can* be different than that. He can be fun!"

"It's been a while since he was fun," Frank said. "I know he's our dad, but sometimes I wish Ma would kick him out."

That had never occurred to Arthur. He didn't want it to happen, even if Frank did. He wondered if his mother would ever do such a thing. He changed the subject.

"I think Nola had fun with me today," he said.

"Did she?"

"Yeah, I think so. *And* she said I was kind of cute."

"That could go either way, to be honest."

"I think she meant it the good way."

"You'd be the judge of that. Trust yourself."

Arthur lay still for a while, thinking of how he was going to be taking Nola to the movies on Saturday night, and then walking her home. In the dark. Suddenly he got a panicky feeling.

"What should I do when I'm walking her home?" he asked Frank.

"Maybe you should brag about your great passion for geography."

"Ha, ha," Arthur said. Geography was another subject that Arthur had difficulty with, practically mixing up Africa with Asia, if not Alabama. "I don't think it's good to brag about anything," he said.

"You're right," Frank said. "A lot of guys brag so often they don't even know they're doing it anymore. They think the natural way is for the conversation to be about nothing but them. If the girl talks, why, it's still about them. You've got to let Nola discover you, and you need to discover her. It becomes an adventure then. For both of you."

"But *how*?"

"*Ask* her things," Frank said, and the tone of his voice made Arthur worry he was getting irritated. Then he reasoned that Frank was just tired; it was late.

Frank punched his pillow and flipped it over. When he lay back down, he spoke quietly. "A guy should ask a girl things like what she wished for most as a child. What she thinks will happen in the future, and what she would like to happen to *her* in the future. Ask her . . . I don't know, just be *curious* about her. Ask her what her favorite color is. What she's scared of most. What kind of people she likes most. But be careful with that one; you can't make her feel like you're pressuring her to say she likes *you*."

"But I think she *does* like me. It's just that we—"

He stopped talking. The stairs up to their bedroom were creaking.

Frank and Arthur went silent. Arthur closed his eyes.

The door banged open. The overhead light went on. Their father shuffled over to Frank's bed.

Arthur said loudly, uselessly, "Hey, Pop!"

Their father grabbed the front of Frank's pajamas and leaned over him. "Guess you have all the answers, huh? Guess you think you're better than me."

"I didn't say that," Frank said, and their dad popped him one.

"You like that? You want some more of that?"

Frank pushed him away, and their dad stumbled and almost fell over. This made him angrier, and he rushed over to Frank and slapped at him. Frank slipped past him and moved across the room to get away, but their father followed him. Frank held his fists over his face protectively, but their dad kept on hitting, and now it was harder.

"Pop!" Arthur cried out, his voice high like a girl's.

He heard a gutteral *ooph!* as their dad socked Frank's midsection. Arthur leaped out of bed and ran over to pull at their father's arm, then started kicking him hard. "*Stop it!*" he yelled. "Pop!"

From behind him, Arthur heard their mother come

into the room. She pushed Arthur aside and tried to separate Frank and her husband. Somehow one of their dad's
punches landed on her, and she fell to the floor, holding
the side of her face. Everyone froze. Then his mom looked
up at his father. "Eugene," she said, and she began to sob.
Her voice cracked as she said, "I *wanted* things!" It made
for the most awful pain inside Arthur.

Their dad made a move toward her but Frank bellowed
like a crazy person and went after him, punching and
punching, his arms like a windmill. Their dad broke free
and ran out of the room, and Frank followed him down
the steps. The back door slammed open and then there
was the sound of them fighting outside.

Arthur's mother got up off the floor and went to the
window. Arthur moved to stand close behind her.

Down below, the two of them were out on the lawn,
still going furiously at each other. It was like watching
wild animals.

"Ma," Arthur said. "We've got to stop them."

She turned and looked at him with a strange kind of
wonderment, then rushed downstairs, Arthur right behind her.

Chapter 8

THE NEXT DAY, after school, Arthur stood outside Miss Arlene's Dress Shop, looking in the window. The mannequins were all wearing beautiful flowered dresses and hats and fancy shoes. He stared up at them, wishing he could go in and buy his mother something, maybe one of the dresses. He had some money in his pocket because he'd been on the way to buy a new model to put together. But now he wanted to do something else.

A bell tinkled when he walked in and a tall woman with wavy blond hair came out from behind some curtains in the back. "Well, hello there!" she said.

Arthur held up his hand in a half wave.

The woman walked over to him. "Are you waiting for your mother?"

"No, ma'am."

"Your dad?"

"No. It's just me. I was just wondering if you could tell me the price of the dress in the window?"

"Which one?"

"The red-flowered one."

"Oh, that's a beauty, isn't it? Everyone looks good in that dress. Is this a gift you're buying?"

"Yes, ma'am."

"What's the occasion?"

The occasion was his mother's eyes, swollen this morning from crying in the night. The occasion was his mother's inability to keep her husband from beating her son, the times when he got in those moods.

Arthur shrugged. "I just wanted to buy something for my mother."

The woman smiled. "Well, isn't that nice! I'd be glad to help you. Let me go and check the price on that dress you wanted."

She climbed into the front window's display space and looked at the little tag tucked inside the dress's sleeve. She called out, "It's five dollars and forty-nine cents."

Arthur swallowed. "Okay. What about the black-and-white dress?"

She climbed out of the window and came to stand before Arthur. "It's about the same price, son." She was beginning to catch on now.

"Maybe just the belt from the red-flowered dress?" Arthur said.

"We don't sell them separately. Sorry."

Arthur looked around the store. "I guess those purses are pretty expensive, too."

"Let's take a look." She went to the wall where the

purses were hung and pulled one down. "Now, this one might be just right for you. It's our flowerpot drawstring model, very popular, and as you can see, it's set off with gold nailheads. It's only two thirty-four. I'm sure your mother would love it."

Arthur didn't know what to do. This had been a stupid idea. He wouldn't be able to afford a dust ball here. He moved closer to the purse and touched it. "Nope," he said.

"No?"

"Nope, it's not right for her."

"Really. Why not? I'm just interested."

"She doesn't like that color."

"We do have them in other colors."

Arthur widened his eyes. "Oh, nuts, I just remembered something. Sorry, I have to go. Thank you!"

He rushed out of the store and down the block. After he turned the corner, he slowed down. That was stupid. Stupid! It was just that he wanted something for his mother, as a way to say that it was okay, everything was okay. When he passed Pearson's Candies, he went in and asked for fifteen cents' worth of fudge. His mother loved fudge. Buying *it* was no problem: the candy was weighed, and then it was put into a nice white bag with a gold logo. Arthur paid for it and had enough money left over for a model. He'd leave the fudge on his mother's pillow for her to find tonight. Maybe then she'd go to bed happy. As for him, he'd lie in bed and dream of his upcoming date.

Chapter 9

FRANK AND ARTHUR had both finished their Saturday jobs early and were sitting at the kitchen table, eating lunch. Arthur's father had been acting subdued and ashamed. He'd said very little to anyone, though just now he'd taken Arthur's mother up to their bedroom, where they spoke quietly for some time. Arthur and Frank tried to eavesdrop, but they couldn't hear anything except for one time when their mother said, "Oh, Eugene, don't you think I *know* that?" Frank and Arthur looked at each other: Know *what*?

When their father came downstairs, he nodded at his sons. "Going out to the barn to tend to Grimy," he said, and neither Arthur nor Frank said anything. It was only after their dad had already gone out the door that Arthur said, "Okay, Pop."

Arthur had just finished eating when his mother came into the room. She'd been crying: there were red splotches on her face and her eyes were still damp.

"Do you want anything else?" she asked Arthur. Her voice had a pinched quality that reminded him of people trying to sound one way when they felt another.

"No, thanks," he said. He put his dishes in the sink.

"Frank?"

"I'm fine, Ma. I'm going out."

She didn't ask where he was going. One reason was that she trusted him. But another, Arthur thought, was that she was just too tired and upset.

Arthur followed Frank outside. "Are you going to see Mary?"

"What do you think?"

"Don't be mad at *me!*"

"Who says I'm mad at you?"

"Well, you're mad."

"That's why I'm going to see Mary." Something occurred to him and he stepped closer to Arthur. "Want to meet me at the tracks later? Say, at two?"

Arthur was afraid to answer. Their dad was *right there;* he could probably hear them. But he nodded at his brother, and Frank took off at a fast walk.

Arthur stood in the yard for a while, looking at the laundry his mother had pegged on the line. He used to lie under that clothesline and watch the sheets billow and think of captains on ships, the wide blue sea, pirates. That would bring no comfort now. What would it be like to be able to go to the one you loved and be comforted, as Frank was now doing? To have someone with whom you could share everything, even the most difficult things? He wanted so much for Nola to be that person. Maybe there'd be a way for him to tell her that tonight.

Just yesterday morning, in school, he'd been at his locker when he'd heard Nola's group of girlfriends talking as they waited for her. The group met every morning near the front entrance, close to where Arthur's locker was. They huddled there talking until the bell rang; then they went their separate ways. After school was over, they met again before they walked home together. Arthur's locker door had been open, blocking their view of him, so they didn't know he was there. He'd flushed when he heard one of them saying, "Oh, come on, I can't believe Nola could like him! Arthur *Moses*?" It was Betty Huron talking. Betty Boop, she was nicknamed, for her flighty ways.

"Well, Doreen Majors and Ducks Tilton saw the two of them together at the soda fountain," another girl said. Arthur believed it was Joan Michaels, head cheerleader of the JV squad, talking, but he didn't want to take the chance of peeking and being discovered.

"She just feels sorry for him," Betty said.

"I don't know," the girl Arthur thought was Joan said. "Even if she did, she certainly doesn't have to—" She stopped talking abruptly to say, "Hi, Nola! You're late today!"

"I know," Nola said breathlessly. "I overslept. I ran practically the whole way here."

The bell had rung then, and Arthur had quickly disappeared into the nearby boys' bathroom. After he thought Nola and her crowd had gone their respective ways, he'd come out and gone to class.

Maybe, he thought, Nola cared more for him than she was able or willing to let on. Maybe he would pop by this afternoon, even if they were going to see each other that night. He might be able to think up some reason to go over there, or make it seem like a coincidence. He would be able to tell if she was looking forward to tonight.

Just as he reached the kitchen door to go back inside, Arthur heard an odd sound coming from the barn, as though someone were hurt. He wasn't sure whether to go and get his mother or to see for himself what it was. He reasoned that his mother had had enough lately, and he headed over himself.

At first he couldn't see anything; it was dark in the barn, even with the sun out. But then he saw his father, slumped down on the floor outside of Grimy's stall. He was crying, making moaning and snuffling sounds. Grimy's head was stretched down low to nuzzle the top of his father's head. Arthur didn't know what to do. His father's legs were drawn up tight against him, his forehead on his knees. He hadn't seen Arthur, so Arthur could leave without his father's knowing. It seemed that might save his pride.

But Frank and Arthur had a theory that if animals liked you—animals or little kids—you couldn't be all bad. When Arthur saw Grimy reaching his head down that way, seemingly trying to comfort his father, the anger he'd been holding on to faded. His dad had one hand up and was rubbing Grimy's muzzle in a way that seemed like he didn't even know he was doing it.

"Pop?"

His father's head snapped up.

"You okay?"

His father's forehead wrinkled as he spread his hand over his face. "I failed her. I failed you all. I never meant . . . I never meant . . ." His shoulders shook with sobbing.

Something happened to Arthur at that point, and it had to do with seeing his father not as his father at all, but as someone else. He saw him simply as a person, struggling, and this made Arthur's heart open. He put his hands in his pockets, leaned forward. "Hey, Pop?"

His father didn't answer, just kept on crying. It was something, seeing a man like him cry. Arthur was beginning to get worried that his mother would hear him, and he knew that would add to his father's pain. He moved closer and sat down on the floor. "Come on, Pop, it wasn't so bad. It was just a fight got out of hand. Everybody's okay."

His dad kept his hand over his face, but Arthur thought he was listening.

Arthur said, "You know what Frank says? He says everything is in everybody: a good man's got plenty of bad in him, and a bad man's got plenty of good."

His dad pulled his hand down and looked over at Arthur. "He said that?"

Arthur nodded, though the answer was no. But Frank *had* told him something the other night, when he was reading from a little Robert Frost book he'd just gotten. He read out a poem called "Birches," and in it was one line that really stuck with Arthur: *Earth's the right place for love.*

And so now Arthur said, "Pop. You know this, but I'm going to tell you anyway. We every one of us love you. We every one of us know that sometimes you just can't say certain things, or that things you do say come out wrong. And that . . ." Arthur hesitated, then said, "You lose your temper quite a bit, and then you say some awful things, and sometimes you hurt us, but you don't really want to."

His father swallowed so hard Arthur heard it. It seemed he was full to the brim, sitting there all bent over with his fists clenched in his lap. Arthur moved closer to him.

Grimy jerked his head up and turned in his stall to yank hay from his feeder. The sound of his chewing was comforting. Sunlight poured in through the high little window of the barn, making for an elongated duplicate on the wooden floor. Arthur watched golden dust motes spin in the air. It wasn't bad, sitting here. Despite everything, it was kind of nice sitting here.

His father leaned back against the stall, crossed his arms, and stared up at the ceiling. He said, "I'll tell you something, Arthur. I had so much I wanted to do for your mother. So much I wanted to give her. And then to you boys. But it seems like everything I try turns out wrong. By now it's almost a habit, maybe even like I *make* things go wrong. A terrible habit that I can't seem to break."

Arthur had a few suggestions, but he thought that for right now, he'd keep them to himself.

His father looked over at him. "It's hard for me to find

a job, Arthur, for lots of reasons. Oh, I know I have a bad attitude, I know I do. But so often . . ." He hesitated, then went on. "So often I'm in a great deal of pain. It takes a lot out of a man to be in such pain. It's not just physical, though I'm here to tell you it *is* physical. But more than that, it's mental. How much I feel like a failure. How I keep slipping further and further behind while all around me guys are doing better and better. I even had a thought to . . . do something illegal."

Arthur eyes grew wide.

"Oh, I'm not going to, but I thought about it. I'm only telling you because it's how desperate I feel. But I'll do better. If there's anything that came out of this . . . out of all that has happened, it's that I'm done being that way. I mean it. I hope you can believe me. Do you, son?"

No, not for one second. Not yet. But Arthur said, "Course I do. And I'll help you, Pop. We all will."

His father nodded.

Arthur didn't want to leave him in the barn alone. "Ma's got lunch for you," he said. "How's about you come inside?"

Arthur stood and watched as his father got up like an old man. Arthur had never seen him move like that. Arthur walked slowly beside him across the yard. The grass was greening in patches, and the damp scent of spring rose up from the earth. The sheets on the line moved like they were waving goodbye.

Arthur thought he knew what his dad had been thinking, sitting out there in the barn. He was thinking that his family would be better off without him. Arthur remembered coming into the living room recently and finding his mother singing along with Vaughn Monroe, *I-I-I-I / wish I / didn't love you so*. When she looked up and saw Arthur, she smiled and shrugged. Frank had begun saying about their father, "It's sad, really." And Arthur, he was thinking . . . What? What was he thinking? He guessed he was thinking, *He's my dad*. He wasn't the most popular guy in the neighborhood. He didn't have a Pepsodent smile and a jaunty stride; he wasn't a member of a bowling league, or a baseball coach, or a Boy Scout troop leader. He wasn't invited to play horseshoes or cards with a bunch of neighborhood men. He didn't take his wife out dancing; he didn't take her out much at all. But he was the one she had chosen, and Arthur didn't believe she was ever going anywhere. And Grimy had nickered after his dad when he left the barn, had watched him walk away with his whole horse heart in his eyes.

Arthur opened the door wide to let them both into the house. His dad went into the kitchen, and Arthur's mom looked over quickly and smiled. She smoothed down the front of her apron and said gently, "Go ahead and wash up, Eugene. I'll fix you a sandwich." Maybe she did wish she didn't love him so, Arthur thought. But what could you do? If nothing else, Arthur had learned this: love came in without knocking and stayed without your permission. And when hard times came between you and the one you loved, you didn't run away. You stayed. His mother had told him that. His mother had *demonstrated* that.

It was getting close to two o'clock, the time he'd agreed to meet Frank at the tracks. Arthur didn't say anything other than "I'm going out." He felt his father's place had changed irrevocably in the family. Frank and Arthur were in charge now.

Chapter 10

"I AM *NOT* A fortune teller," the skinny woman with long gray braids told Arthur, once the two of them had hoisted themselves up into the boxcar. Her fingers were bony and misshapen, and she had sunken-in places behind her collarbones so deep they looked like you could keep things there. The skin on her face was thin and blotchy, and she had the kind of eyes that shifted color: brown, green, back to brown. Her front teeth were missing, and her lips were dry and cracked. Still, when she smiled, Arthur thought it looked like a bow on a present. He'd never seen anyone like her, and he studied her in a way he hoped wasn't too obvious. She wore a battered brown fedora, men's shoes, and jeans that were belted with a length of clothesline. Her red-and-white striped T-shirt had seen better days, but it was clean, and Arthur thought it looked nice on her. Her tan jacket was tied around her waist; the day was unusually warm even with the breeze. She had a length of thin rawhide around her neck, with something that looked like bones and feathers hung on it. Arthur didn't want to look too closely at that; it was like the owl pellets Frank had shown him once, things the owl had eaten and couldn't digest: teeth, claws, feathers, even tiny skulls.

Frank was outside the boxcar with some of the guys who were hanging around the tracks that day. He seemed to know some of them well. Arthur didn't want Frank to leave him here alone; these people were a little scary. But it didn't seem like Frank was going anywhere; he was lying on the ground and leaning back on his elbows, talking and laughing.

The woman opened a banged-up suitcase she was carrying, *Lady* something or other written on it in a mostly chipped-off gold foil. She shook out a neatly folded army blanket and laid it down for Arthur and her to sit on. Arthur sat cross-legged opposite her and laughed, though he had no idea why. Nerves, maybe.

"What's funny?" the woman asked.

"Nothing."

"You nervous?"

"Yes."

"Relax," she said. "I ain't going to hurt you. Unless you're one of them that the truth hurts. Are you one of them?"

"No, ma'am. I don't think so."

"Well, relax, then."

Arthur loosened his shoulders and looked around. The

boxcar seemed surprisingly big to him, and he figured it was because he'd never been in one, or even close to one. Hay was stuck in the corners, and the scent of manure was in the air, even with the sliding door open all the way. Arthur liked the smell of manure, and he thought a lot of other people did, too, but they didn't like to admit it, same as they didn't like to say they enjoyed a good burp. But who didn't?

"You're not a fortune teller?" Arthur asked. "Frank said you were."

"Yeah, that's what Frank calls me, a 'fortune teller.' That's not right. What I am is a clairvoyant. There's a big difference. When people say 'fortune teller,' they're mostly talking about charlatans running around wearing turbans, with upside-down goldfish bowls that they stare into to make up pure bullshit. No. I got a gift. Have since I was a girl. I just *know* things. My grandmother was the same, and she was famous, too; her name was Frieda Swanson. Ever hear of her?"

Arthur wondered why she would ask him. Wouldn't she *know* if he had? But, "No," he said. "I don't believe I have."

"My people aren't from here, that's why," she said. "If you lived in the Dayton area, you'd know her all right. Some folks were afraid of her, like she was a witch or something. But all she did was tell people the truth, and that's what I do. Not terrible news or violent deaths; I don't tell people if I see that coming for them. What good would it do? They'd just worry about it until it happened.

My grandmother foretold a death one time, and somebody got all riled up and decided she was a murderer. She
got run out of town. She left with nothing but what she
was wearing."

"I'm sorry."

"Ha! Don't be! She went clear to San Francisco, and
she was a *star* there, I'm telling you. People lining up to
see her. Ringling Brothers asked her did she want to join
up with them, but of course she said no. It's not a parlor
trick, the gift of seeing; it's a gift from God. But she
stayed in San Francisco and lived in great comfort until
she died. She had herself a peignoir with feather-boa
trim, and satin high-heeled slippers. She had a mink stole
and a diamond necklace, too. Spread that on your toast
and eat it!"

Arthur wanted to ask this woman why she wasn't in
San Francisco herself, why she lived what looked to be a
pretty hard life, but it wasn't his business. People didn't
always choose what you thought they should.

"All right, let's get started," the woman said. "You got
the money?"

Arthur gave it to her, and she stashed it in her pocket.
Then she took a deep breath and stared into Arthur's face
so deep and long he wanted to look away, but he didn't.
He'd paid the fifty cents. He'd take whatever was coming.

The woman closed her eyes. "N," she said, softly. "I'm
getting the letter N. Does that have any significance for
you?" She scratched at her elbow, staring at Arthur.

Nola! Arthur thought. *Holy smokes!*

"Yes, ma'am," he said excitedly. "N stands for—"

"Don't tell me. I tell *you*. Okay? That's how it works here. I tell you. You keep your trap shut, that's your job."

Arthur nodded, and the woman closed her eyes again.

"Well," she said after a few minutes. "You got a bit of a rough ride ahead." She opened her eyes. "You know what a maze is, right?"

Arthur nodded.

"It's going to be like that with this girl you're stuck on. A lot of dead ends."

The disappointment must have shown on his face, because she said loudly, "Take heart!"

Arthur said nothing.

"Did you hear me?"

Arthur spoke softly, trying to split the difference between keeping his trap shut and answering the question. "Yes, ma'am," he said.

"This girl N is pretty knotted up inside. She's not a bad girl, by which I mean she's kind. But she's like a little kid, distracted by shiny, meaningless things. You want me to tell you what I see will happen between you in the end?"

Arthur thought that had been the point of the fifty cents, which he *could* have used to help buy a model of the Curtiss Jenny biplane for him and Frank to put together. But now he wondered whether he wanted to hear this woman's prediction. She had said she didn't like to tell people really bad news, so it couldn't be too awful. But what he really cared about was what was happening *now*. If he knew what was happening now, maybe he could shape the future despite what the woman might think she saw.

He sat deliberating, when from outside he heard some-one yell, "Cops!"

The woman jumped to her feet, grabbed her suitcase, and snatched the blanket out from under Arthur so hard he almost somersaulted. Then she leaped out the door of the boxcar and went running into the woods.

Arthur didn't know what to do. Outside, people were milling around and talking loud, gathering up their things and running. He couldn't see Frank anywhere.

He stood at the edge of the boxcar and looked down. The ground was far away; the car seemed higher now than when he'd pulled himself up there.

Then there was Frank, yelling his name, running toward him. "Jump!" he said. "We gotta *go!*"

Arthur looked to see if there was a way he could easily climb down. There was nothing he might be able to hold on to. Then he heard a loud clanking sound, and the box-car started to move. He jumped, and he fell when he landed. Frank ran over and scooped him up like a football, and they lit out of there.

Once they were clear of the yard, they both broke up laughing. It was relief, that was all. Arthur didn't even know why they had run. What would the cops have done, anyway? He and Frank weren't doing anything wrong. He asked why they'd have gotten into trouble if they hadn't run, and the smile disappeared from his brother's face.

"Loitering," Frank said. "That's one of the things that

gets hung on those people all the time. They'd accuse us of the same thing. Pop would go nuts."

"We weren't loitering," Arthur said. "I had a business appointment."

That set them to laughing again, and then Frank said, "So what did she tell you?"

"Well, for one thing, she said she's not a fortune teller."

"Is that so?" Frank was still a little out of breath.

"That's right. She's a clairvoyant."

"I don't see what the difference is. Did she tell you what's going to happen on your date with Nola tonight?"

Arthur's stomach tightened. "No."

"Do *you* know what's going to happen on your date with Nola tonight?"

"How would *I* know?"

Frank punched him lightly on the arm. "Come on, Arthur. This is the part where you show some confidence. This is where you say, 'Course I do. I'm going to kiss her so good it'll make her swoon!'"

Arthur smiled. "Yeah. Sure."

Frank stopped walking. "Say, you've . . . Have you ever kissed a girl, Arthur?"

Peggy Miller, when they were about four. Outside in the bushes one summer day. Arthur kissed her and she ran away, screaming. Not much of a morale booster.

"Course I have," Arthur said, but the tone of his voice gave him away.

"Need any pointers?"

"Like what?"

Frank didn't answer. He stopped walking and looked up at the sky. Arthur saw that it had turned a weird greenish color and lightning was flashing. Then there came a distant roaring sound, almost like another kind of train.

"Tornado!" Frank said, and they raced the short distance home. When they got to the house, they saw their father standing at the entrance of the storm cellar. "Get in!" he yelled, waving his arm frantically. Frank and Arthur scuttled down the wooden steps and onto the dirt floor, and their father slammed the door shut just in time.

Their mother grabbed Frank and Arthur, saying, "Oh, thank God, thank God." They could barely hear her over the sound of the wind and the banging of debris flying around. They all stood looking up, though they could see nothing. No one spoke, but Arthur felt he knew what they were all thinking: *If only I can get out of this alive . . .* And then what? When you thought your life was in danger, things could get very clear: What you wanted. What you didn't. The things you'd done right, the things you'd done wrong. How you were going to shape things going forward, *if only you could survive.* Arthur had been in the storm cellar before; on more than one occasion he had had doubts that his family *would* survive. But thus far the tornadoes had ended and out they'd all come. Out they'd come into a day gone quiet, and they'd gone back to normal, and they'd considered themselves lucky that they *could* do that. But Arthur thought that when that happened, something had been lost, some opportunity. He figured most people were like him: they didn't act on the things they'd promised themselves in times of great fear. Oh, things might change for a day or two, but then, almost always, things went back to the way they had been. Arthur thought it was odd that only in extreme danger, or maybe on your deathbed, could you achieve a certain kind of surety about what mattered most in your life. But now, standing and looking up at the rattling storm door with his family gathered close around him in the darkness, Arthur made a promise he intended never to break. And that promise was never to deny love. He wasn't thinking only of Nola when he made this promise; he was thinking of life itself, of the bounty it offered and of the bounty he could return.

Tornadoes could last for a long time. This one didn't, though, and very soon it was quiet. Their father went up the steps of the storm cellar and cautiously opened the door a bit, then flung it open all the way. There was the blue sky, innocent-seeming, like nothing at all had happened. And then they heard their father cry out.

Arthur's mom raced up the stairs and Frank and Arthur followed. When they cleared the cellar, they saw the damage: the house appeared to be fine, but one side of the barn had collapsed. The chickens that weren't dead were running around hysterically. Their dad walked over to the partially fallen structure and stood still, leaning forward to peer inside. He turned around and his face was stony. "Grimy's not here."

He moved closer to the barn and picked up a long piece of wood. Arthur saw eggs smashed all over, nest boxes piled up on top of one another. Arthur's dad held on to the piece of wood for a moment, then tossed it back onto the ground. He looked at Arthur's mother and spoke softly. "I don't know." He shook his head. "Cripes."

"We're safe, Eugene," she said. "That's all that matters."

They all helped to pile up the bigger pieces of the barn that could be used in rebuilding, and then they went inside the house to make sure everything was all right there. Arthur figured that afterward they'd go out into the neighborhood as they always did after something like this happened, seeing if they could help someone who'd gotten it worse than they had. Nobody said anything about Grimy. Arthur figured there was a chance the horse had just spooked and run, and they'd find him. When the family ventured back outside, Frank headed in the direction of Mary's house.

"Where are you going?" their mother called after him.

"Just in this direction, to see if folks are okay."

Nola! Arthur thought. He told his parents he'd be right back and went into the house to call her. Thankfully, the phone was working fine, and he got through.

Nola answered, and Arthur said, "Are you okay?"

". . . Who is this?'

"Oh. It's Arthur. Arthur Moses? I just was calling to see if you were all right."

"Yes, we're all right. Sounds like you are, too. Gosh. Isn't it awful?"

"I guess we can't go to the movies."

"No, I know. The house a few doors down from us got hit pretty bad. We were just going over there."

"We're doing that, too. Going out to help. I'm awful sorry about the movies, though."

"Oh, for heaven's sake, Arthur! We had a *tornado*! I have to go."

"Me, too," Arthur said, but Nola had already hung up.

He caught up with his parents and they walked around the neighborhood. It looked like most people had escaped with minimum damage, or with no damage at all. But the Kiersons had lost everything: their house was flattened. Folks had gathered in their yard, trying hard not to gawk too much. Some of the men had shovels, and one had a chain saw. Mrs. Kierson was sobbing in her husband's arms. They were a young couple, and Arthur saw that Mrs. Kierson had a baby on the way. He imagined they were grateful they were alive, but look at their house. Such a private thing, Arthur thought, that kind of grief; everyone had to look away. But everyone also stayed there, to offer what they could. As soon as the Kiersons got hold of themselves, folks would begin looking for what could be salvaged, sorting various things into piles. Arthur stared at the absurd sight of a toilet standing right out in the open.

At six o'clock, Arthur and his parents headed home. They found Frank in the kitchen, sitting at the kitchen table. Arthur could tell by the ease in his expression that Mary had been okay.

"What's for dinner around here?" Frank asked. "I'm starving!"

Their mother shook her finger at him, but she was smiling.

They were just sitting down to deviled ham sandwiches when their dad bolted out the door. Trotting down the street was Grimy, pretty as you please, head up proud like he was at the head of a parade. They all ran outside, laughing and calling, "Grimy! Grimy!" and their dad hugged the little horse hard around the neck. "I don't know where I'll put him," he said, looking around the yard, where there was a lot left to clean up.

"Bring him in the house!" Arthur said, and of course he was joking.

But that is exactly what their dad did. He brought Grimy into the kitchen while they all ate dinner. The worst did not happen, which is to say that Grimy did not evacuate, nor did the floorboards give way. The horse just stood placidly, watching them eat, and when their mother had finished, she gave Grimy an apple and a carrot and called him sweetheart. Their dad found a clearing for him outside and tethered him to a tree. That night, their father brought a blanket and pillow outside so that he could sleep on the ground next to Grimy. In the morning, he started in on repairing the barn wall, and Frank and Arthur helped.

Chapter 11

"I DON'T TRUST IT," Frank said. He and Arthur were lying in their beds and Arthur was telling Frank about what had transpired in the barn between their dad and him. Arthur didn't want to reveal everything, like his dad crying; it seemed that in spite of everything, he owed his father a little privacy, some dignity. But he had told Frank a lot. For his part, Frank said he'd noticed the way their dad had been gentler toward all of them, more subdued. How he'd made a point of thanking Arthur and Frank for helping him sort debris from the barn, salvaging what they could to rebuild.

"But he's done this before," Frank said. "He stops drinking completely, he gets on the straight and narrow, then something happens, and he's right back at it."

Arthur considered this. He guessed it was true, though it had to be acknowledged that one of the reasons their dad went off on Frank was mostly because of the way

Frank liked to provoke him. "But did Pop ever spill his guts out like that to you?" Arthur asked.

"No."

"Well, doesn't it seem like that's the start of something different?"

"I don't know. Maybe you're right. Maybe he's reached some breaking point. What would help most is if he'd just get a job, you know? He could do an office job!"

"Maybe he'll get one," Arthur said, and he wished so hard he could do something to make that happen. But what could he do? If Arthur were a character in a movie, he could. He'd be in some random place, like the soda shop; maybe he'd be working there with a white paper hat on his head. And in would walk some big-shot business guy and he'd sit at the counter and take off his hat and order a Black Cow, and he and Arthur would get to talking, and the guy would say he sure wished he could find a good man to hire. But things didn't happen in real life like they did in the movies. And, anyway, you had to be careful about making suggestions to their father. He was more likely than not to take it the wrong way.

Frank whispered something urgent-sounding.

"What?" Arthur whispered back.

"*Shhh!* Listen!"

When Arthur fell silent, he heard the faint sounds of bed springs creaking coming from their parents' bedroom. He did not want to hear that, and Frank knew it. Frank thought it was funny to listen whenever that happened, but Arthur was of another mind.

"It's not your business!" he whispered angrily to Frank, the sides of his pillow pulled up over his ears.

"A *whip*-poor-will?" Frank asked.

Arthur listened again, and now he heard the kind of excited, kind of whistling sound of the night bird. Well, spring was coming on full force now, if the whip-poor-wills were out. Arthur knew some things about the mythology surrounding the bird. If it sang near a house, it might foretell death, or at least bad luck. And it was said you could cure an aching back if you turned somersaults to the whippoorwill's call. He told Frank that.

"Seriously?" Frank asked.

"Yup."

"How do you know that?"

"Well, I don't *know* it. It's a myth."

"But how do you know about the myth?"

"My bird book." Arthur said it lightly, as if knowing such things were as easy as pie. It *was* easy to learn such things. Of course, first you had to have an interest in the natural world, as Arthur always had. It was nice that he finally knew something Frank didn't.

Arthur crossed his arms behind his head and his tone grew expansive. "There are a lot of myths surrounding that bird," he said. "Like that it's one of the gods of the night and can turn a frog into the moon. And that moccasin flowers are the shoes of whip-poor-wills."

"Shoes!"

"Yup. And here's a good one: whip-poor-wills drink milk from she-goats."

Arthur waited for Frank's reaction to that one, but it was quiet.

"Frank?" he finally whispered.

"What." His brother's tone was strange, angry-seeming.

"What's wrong?"

Frank raised himself up on his elbows. "Can you keep a secret?"

"Of course."

"I mean it, Arthur, you can't tell anyone. 'Cause I don't know what I'm going to do yet."

"About what?" Frank was making Arthur kind of nervous now.

"Mary's pregnant."

Arthur nearly fell out of his bed.

"She is?"

"Yes."

"Are you sure?"

"Yeah."

"How bad off is she?"

"I don't think that's quite the way to put it."

"I just mean how far along."

"We figure two and a half months."

Arthur's mind was racing. But he tried to speak calmly so Frank wouldn't feel worse. "Well, you said you were going to marry her."

"Yeah, I did."

"So . . ."

"I don't know, Arthur. It's different now. I mean, going

off to New York City the way I wanted to—I just don't see how we can do that now."

"Why not? You'd just live there 'stead of here. Right?"

"It's a lot harder to live there. You need more money. And . . . I guess it makes me sound like a creep to say this, but I was counting on her supporting *me* until I could support *her*. That's what she said. She said she'd teach and I'd write, and after I got to publishing books, then she'd stay home. Or maybe keep up with her teaching job. We didn't ever even *talk* about kids."

"You mean about if you wanted them?"

"Right."

"You don't want them?"

"I didn't say that. I don't know. I don't know!"

"Are you going to get married right away?"

"Everything is just different now. I guess I'm kind of . . . I keep putting it out of my head. It's hard to think about what to do. But I'm responsible for two people now. For a kid *and* Mary! I just didn't figure on this." He lay flat again.

After a while, Arthur said, "You'll figure it out, Frank. You'll be okay. You all will. You still love her, right?"

Frank didn't answer. Arthur wished he could think of the right thing to say or do. But sometimes all you could do was let someone know you cared, and then let them find their own solutions. He turned over and let Frank be.

Chapter 12

ARTHUR WAS HAVING a discouraging after-school meeting with his math teacher. "I think you're just not trying hard enough," Mrs. Enos said, Arthur's D– test between them.

"I *do* try," Arthur said. "I try really hard, but I just don't get it."

Mrs. Enos regarded him over the top of her thin wire glasses. "Tell me about how you try."

"Well, I look at the problems real slow. Then I wait a bit and look at them again."

"And?" Mrs. Enos said.

"That's the funny part. Seems like the more I look at them, the harder they get."

Mrs. Enos sat back in her chair. She was wearing a black-and-white polka-dot dress and a pin with cherries hanging down. Arthur liked that pin, and he wished they could talk about it. But no, they had to talk about how poorly he was doing in algebra.

"I wonder, Arthur," Mrs. Enos said, "if you're trying *too* hard. I wonder if you'd just relax a little and start your work with the idea that you're going to do *just fine,* if it wouldn't make a difference."

Outside the window were the bleachers next to the football field. Arthur saw a lone figure climbing up to the top row, then sitting down. Nola McCollum. She put her books beside her and leaned her head back, her face tilted up toward the sun. This would be a perfect opportunity to ask her out to the movies again. He hadn't had the nerve to call her again after her brusque dismissal of him when he'd checked up on her after the tornado.

"Arthur?" Mrs. Enos said.

Arthur snapped his attention back to his teacher. "Yes, ma'am?"

"Will you give it a try?"

"Relaxing, you mean?" he asked.

"Yes. Just come to your work with the idea that it will be easy! Maybe even fun! Will you try that for me, Arthur?"

"I guess I could try. I *will* try." He began to gather up his books, and Mrs. Enos put her hand on his arm.

"I want to tell you, Arthur, that this is our last resort. I've tried to help you in every other way I can think of. If you continue to do this poorly, you'll need to repeat this class next year."

"Okay. Thanks, Mrs. Enos."

He walked out of the classroom as quickly as he could and still be polite. He liked Mrs. Enos, and he thought she liked him. She was just trying to help. And maybe she was right; maybe relaxing a little around algebra *would* help. Maybe relaxing around a certain someone would help, too.

When he reached the bleachers, he began walking down the well-worn path in front of them as though he didn't know Nola was there. He was hoping she'd call out to him. But she didn't. He snuck a look over and saw her still sitting with her face to the sun. She hadn't seen him.

He coughed.

Nothing.

"Hey, Nola!" he shouted. His heart was beating fast. *Relax,* he thought.

Nola sat up and shaded her eyes. "Oh, hi, Arthur. What are you doing?"

"Just going home," he said. "Taking a shortcut." Luckily, Nola had no idea where he lived.

"Can I come up there?" he asked.

"Sure."

When Arthur reached the top bleacher, he sat beside Nola. "Hi," he said, and tried to will away the heat he could feel rising up into his face, tried to disguise the fact that he was winded.

"What are you doing up here?" he asked.

"Oh, just . . . imagining a football game."

"Really?"

"No. I don't even like football. I like being a cheerleader, but I don't like football. All that grunting and groaning and piling up on each other. All that whistle blowing and time-outs and 'First in ten, do it again!'"

"Right. It's not *my* sport," Arthur said. "Although I guess I'd have to say no sport is my sport. I *have* been thinking about trying out for the AV squad." A rush of doubt now: maybe he shouldn't have said that; maybe it wasn't funny.

But it seemed she hadn't heard him. She was staring straight ahead, somber-faced.

"Nola?"

"Yes?" She brightened immediately and looked over at him, but it was a false brightness; her eyes gave her away. Her eyes and her clenched fists.

"I hope you won't mind my asking such a personal question, but are you upset about something?"

She stared into her lap. "Not upset, really. More like I'm just . . . *tired* of some things."

He waited.

"I just . . ." She looked into his face, as though trying to calculate something. "I guess I feel like everybody thinks I'm so lucky. But lately I don't feel so lucky. I feel confused."

"What are you confused about?"

"*Everything.*" She looked away from him.

He wasn't sure what to say. Finally, "Yeah," he said, nodding, trying to convey some sense of understanding. And it seemed to work, because now Nola spoke again.

"You know what my favorite animal is?" she asked him.

"Dog?"

"Nope."

"Tarantula?"

"Goodness! Nope, it's a turtle."

"Really! What do you like about them?" Arthur asked.

"First of all, their faces," she said. "So wise-seeming, so patient. Don't you think so, Arthur?"

"I *do* think so. I've always thought so, though I've never said it. They look like good old grandpas to me."

"Exactly! So peaceful. But what I really like is how un-*perturbed* they always seem. Just going along at their own pace, not seeming to pay any attention to what anyone else is doing. I wish I could be that way. I'm so aware all the time of what other people are thinking. Of me, I mean. I guess that sounds conceited."

"Oh, no, Nola. Everybody worries about what others think of them."

"Do you?"

He thought about this. He guessed there was only one person whose opinion of him he worried about, that being the lovely girl sitting beside him, her hair blowing in the breeze, her lips so pink and pretty.

But, "Sure I do," he said.

"Huh," she said. "I guess I always thought of you as, I don't know . . . a turtle!"

Arthur grimaced.

She put her hand on his arm. "Not in a bad way! I just mean that you seem sort of wise to me. Not so concerned about *Well, how popular am I to*day?"

"Is that what you worry about, Nola?"

"No, not . . ." She pulled her hand away and sat thinking. Finally, she said, "Well, yes. It's embarrassing to admit, but I do worry about how popular I am. It's as though I'm always trying to stay in a certain place. And I don't even know if it's a place I really want to be. I'm beginning to wonder if I'm in the wrong group of people. There's so much pressure to wear the right thing, be seen in the right places, go out with the right boys. What these people talk about doesn't seem to have any substance really, not for me. But I'm afraid to change the topic of conversation to something I find interesting." She sighed. "I don't know, Arthur. I feel like a girl trying to decide whether or not to break up with a boy, but instead of a boy, it's a whole crowd of people. But they are my friends, truly they are!"

"I know one thing," Arthur said.

"What?"

"You don't have to decide anything right now. It's like that filmstrip they showed us last week. At this age, we're supposed to be weighing options, figuring out what's right."

"You mean that one we saw in health sciences?" Nola asked. *"The Turbulent Times of the Teenage Years?"* She rolled her eyes.

"Yes. But it's true, isn't it, what it said?"

"I guess so." Nola looked at her watch. "I've got to go, table-setting time." She stood, straightened her skirt, gathered her books, and smiled at Arthur. "Thank you," she said. "Gosh, you're so . . . Well, I just . . . *Thank* you."

"You're welcome. And Nola?"

"Yes?"

"You're not the only one with problems. Just before I came out here, I was being chewed out by Mrs. Enos for almost flunking math."

"Oh, who cares about math?" Nola said.

They smiled at each other, and then she walked down the steps while Arthur sat watching her go. He wished he'd managed to ask her to the movies. Still, he felt like he'd made some progress.

Chapter 13

ON SATURDAY, WHEN Arthur came down for breakfast, Frank had left for work at the grocery store, and his father was gone, too. It was just Arthur and his mother, something he always liked. She poured Arthur a glass of orange juice and set down a bowl of Cheerios. "Your dad's on the way to an interview," she said. "He's going to talk to someone about a job."

"Doing what?"

"Selling Kirby vacuums, door-to-door. I guess it's a pretty good job, but he'd be gone four days a week. He'd leave on Monday, come home on Friday."

Arthur spoke around a mouthful of cereal. "That would be great!" No more walking on eggshells every minute, wondering what might set his dad off.

But he instantly regretted his words. It might be nice for him and Frank to have their father gone a lot, but his mother would probably look at it differently. "I mean the job, you know. I'll bet he could make some decent money."

"I guess," Arthur's mother said. "And he'd get a car."

"Wowser! Really?"

"Uh-huh." She went over to the sink and stood there, her back to him. She wasn't washing dishes; she was just standing there.

"Can I have some more cereal?" Arthur asked.

Most of the time, if you asked for more of something, his mother would ask if you were *really* still hungry, and Arthur was all prepared with his answer: he had a job today that was going to last until five o'clock. It was sweeping up hair at Mrs. Nelson's beauty parlor, which was off the living room of her house. His mother went there once in a blue moon, as she said, to get her hair cut and curled. Arthur always thought she looked like a million bucks when she came out of there, though he never told her so. Nobody did, including his dad, but you could tell that she was pleased with herself on those days, and she knew that even if the men in her house didn't comment on her improved appearance, they noticed it, all right.

His mother came over to the table and sat down. She took a sip from the fresh cup of coffee she'd poured herself.

"Can I?" Arthur asked.

She looked at him.

"*May* I," he said.

"May you what?"

"Have more cereal?"

"Sure."

That was easy, Arthur thought, and overfilled the bowl a bit.

"Arthur?"

Uh-oh. He would put some back.

But it wasn't that. "I have something to tell you." She smiled at him. Arthur smiled back uncertainly.

"You had a telephone call this morning."

"I did? How come you didn't wake me up?"

"I tried to, but you were sound asleep. I'll bet you and Frank were up till all hours again."

Arthur looked down into his cereal bowl and grunted. Acknowledgment or denial, it could go either way.

"I took a message," his mother said. "It was from a young lady."

Now Arthur looked up quickly.

"A Nola McCollum?" she said.

Paralysis.

"She wanted to know if you could meet her at the park by the river this afternoon. At the old band shell."

"Well, I . . . I have to *work* until five!" Now he was mad that he'd agreed to that job. Sweeping up hair! When he could be with Nola! But he couldn't back out now. He was due there in half an hour.

"I took the liberty of telling her that," his mother said. "And she said she'd meet you *after* five." She raised her eyebrows and smiled. He guessed she was teasing him a bit.

"She's just a friend," Arthur said.

"Well, that's nice. It's nice to have a friend who's a girl."

"*Any*way," Arthur said. He was trying to be calm, but he thought his excitement must be showing.

His mother leaned in closer to him. She said, "You know, Arthur, I once had a picnic with a fellow at that same place."

"Did you?" Good. They were off on another subject, and besides that, he really liked it when she told him stories about men she'd known in the past.

"Yes. He knew how much I liked picnics; I guess I'd told him that. Anyway, he wanted to surprise me, and he invited me one Saturday morning to take a walk with him to the park. When we got there, it was just about lunchtime, and he said, 'Boy, I'm awful hungry. Are you?' I said I was, even though I wasn't, because by then I knew he had some sort of surprise planned."

"And women like surprises," Arthur said.

"Yes. I think most people do. Anyway, we walked along a bit more and then he stopped and pointed to a bush and said, 'What the heck is under *there*?' I thought it was a wild animal or something. Maybe a dead animal. I grabbed his arm and we moved closer, very slowly, and then he bent down and yanked out a *picnic* hamper. Well, I just started laughing. I was so relieved and delighted, but he thought I was making fun of him, laughing that way. 'No, no,' I said, 'this is just wonderful!' He had a blanket in there, too, and peanut-butter-and-jelly sandwiches, and an apple and a Hershey bar to share. It was awfully cute.

"We had just started to eat when it began to rain, one of those sudden squalls. We ran under the gazebo and spread the blanket out there. When I unwrapped my sandwich from the wax paper, I saw a big black ant stuck in the jelly."

"What'd you do?" Arthur was thinking she probably jumped up and screamed.

"I ate it."

"You ate the *ant*?"

"I swallowed pretty quickly."

"Did the guy notice?"

"No. There were no ants on his sandwich, I guess."

"But why would you take a chance on eating an *ant*? It could have killed you or something!"

"Oh, for heaven's sake, Arthur, eating an ant won't kill you."

"But why didn't you tell him?"

"Well, because I knew how much it had meant to him, this picnic. How he'd planned it all out to be such a nice surprise. Then the rain came and he was so disappointed. And kind of embarrassed, like the weather was his fault. I wasn't going to complain about an ant and ruin it even more for him."

"So who was that one?" Arthur asked, and his mother said, "*That* one was your father."

Arthur sat still. Then he said, "Huh."

His mother said, "I think we should give him a chance, don't you? This job might be all he needs." She looked at the kitchen clock. "You'd better go. Do a good job; she's paying you five dollars."

Arthur stopped midway from rising up in his chair. "Really?"

"Really."

He ran out the door, then back in. "Bye, Ma!"

She turned around and smiled at him, and Arthur thought she looked so pretty. Like a girl surprised by a picnic. "See you at supper," she said. "Have *fun!*"

When Arthur got to the beauty shop, Mrs. Nelson welcomed him like he was her long-lost son. She was one of those overly friendly types who squished people into her bosom and nearly suffocated them every time she met up with them. "I'm so glad you could come!" she said.

"Yes, ma'am." Out of the corner of his eye, Arthur saw a line of women sitting near the wall in swivel chairs, three of them. They were all getting their hair cut. Across from them, against the opposite wall, were a couple of other women who looked like a science experiment. They were sitting under big metal hoods that were roaring away. The women had cotton behind their ears and netting over their curlers, and they were reading magazines or talking loudly to each other to be heard. They seemed happy enough, Arthur thought, but he sure wouldn't have wanted to be under a machine that looked like it could electrocute you if you spit sideways. Here was yet another time he was glad he was male. The fussing women felt they had to do!

Mrs. Nelson gave Arthur a big long-handled broom and a dustpan. "Now, the job is pretty simple, Arthur. What I want you to do is sweep up any hair that falls from the women getting a cut, even the little, tiny pieces." She pointed to a closed door. "You can put it in the trash can that's back there, but be sure you keep that door closed except to go in and out. We don't need to subject our customers to what goes on behind the scenes. It's also very important that you don't disturb our stylists when they're working; you can't interfere with their concentration. They're creating works of art the same as a painter, only they're doing it with a comb and scissors. The reason I got rid of the boy I hired before is that he just couldn't seem to understand that, how important a hair stylist is to a woman. Why, Joan Crawford herself said that next to talent, the most important thing for a star to have is a good hair stylist. It isn't only movie stars who feel that way. I make it a personal mission to have every woman who comes in here feel like she's walking on air when she leaves."

That part Arthur knew was true. "My mom sure does love coming here."

"I know she does. I only wish she could come more often; she truly enjoys it here. So, anyway, when the stylist is all done cutting, she'll walk the client over to the dryer. Then, and *only* then, do you sweep. Okay?"

"Okay."

He started to move to a chair someone had just vacated when Mrs. Nelson called his name.

"Ma'am?" he said, trying not to let any irritation show. Cripes, he understood the job!

"There's a lunch all made up for you in the back," she said. "You can help yourself to it whenever you get hungry."

Now Arthur felt ashamed. But he recovered pretty quickly. Five bucks and a free lunch—you couldn't beat that. Even better, he'd be meeting Nola later.

Chapter 14

BY THE TIME five o'clock rolled around, Arthur was dead on his feet. It was true that Frank and he had stayed up late talking. In addition to that, sweeping was harder than he'd thought it would be: those tiny pieces stuck to everything! He hadn't sat down once, not even to eat his lunch, which was sensational. He'd bolted down salami and cheese on rye. A pickle. An orange. Three butter cookies. That was a better lunch than he ever got at home.

Mrs. Nelson thanked him effusively and paid him for coming. "See you next week?" he asked.

Now her expression changed. "I surely do appreciate your helping out today, Arthur, but I think it's best if I find someone else to help out regularly." She was speaking in hushed tones now, as though they were in church.

"Did I do something wrong?"

"It's just that you made some of the women uncomfortable, staring at them the way you did."

Arthur was embarrassed. But he hadn't stared at all the

women. He'd stared at one, who had looked to him like a grown-up Nola: black hair and blue eyes, skin like poured milk. She'd sat in the chair under the dryer, and every time she looked up, she'd smiled at Arthur. So he hadn't thought she'd minded him looking at her a little, though in truth it was more than a little. Basically, times when he wasn't sweeping, he held on to his broom in the corner of the room and looked over at her. And here was the kicker: her husband came to pick her up and he was nothing to see, at *all*. He wasn't even as tall as she was, and his hair was thinning something fierce. But he came to get her, and she took his arm and thanked Mrs. Nelson. How did he *get* her? Arthur wondered.

"I'm sorry," he told Mrs. Nelson.

"It's all right, Arthur."

It was when Arthur was about halfway to the park to meet Nola that he realized the beautiful woman probably hadn't been thanking Mrs. Nelson when she left. Why would she pull her close and whisper in her ear to thank her? No, she'd probably been saying something like "You might want to speak to that boy. He wouldn't stop staring at me."

Well, it was over and done with, and Arthur had money in his pocket and was on his way to meet another beauty. But when he came upon Nola, she was sitting on the floor of the gazebo, her back against a pillar, and crying.

"Nola?"

"Arthur! Oh, jeez." She wiped at her face. "I'm sorry."

Arthur sat next to her. "Don't be sorry. What's wrong?"

"I'm not even telling you. It's too dumb." She jumped

up. "Let's go down by the water. I'm just itching to get my feet in there!"

"But, Nola—"

"Come on!" She ran ahead of him.

Once they were seated on the bank of the river, Nola said, "Well, here goes." She took her shoes off, then her socks, which she stuffed into her shoes. Arthur guessed maybe he shouldn't be watching, but *holy smokes*.

Nola put her shoes behind her and scooched closer to the water. Over her shoulder, she said, "If I had my way, I'd go barefoot all the time. Unless there was snow."

She pushed her feet into the water, squealed, and took them back out. Then she put them in again. "Mind over matter," she said.

Arthur moved closer to the water. And to her, of course—but not too close. Frank had told him, *You don't jump a girl like a clod. You move slowly.*

"Take your shoes and socks off, Arthur," Nola said.

"Nah." Arthur crossed his arms over his raised knees and stared straight ahead. He squinted his eyes a little to look mannish.

"Why won't you put your feet in?" Nola's blue eyes were on him like the prettiest headlights.

"I don't know." Arthur laughed. A stupid laugh. A *chuckle*, like an old man would do.

"Are you . . . ? Arthur. Are you *shy* about it?"

"No!" *Yes.*

Nola clasped her hands together beneath her chin. "How adorable. You are adorable!"

"It's just . . . I don't have the best-looking feet."

"I don't, either!" She pulled her feet from the water. "Look at that!"

"No, you've got really pretty feet, Nola." Those pinkish toenails, like the inside of seashells.

Arthur cleared his throat. He wanted to shove his hands into his pockets. He wanted to hide his face. But he had to learn to take chances, like Frank had told him. So he made himself look right at Nola. "Fact, everything about you is pretty."

Nola looked down, her smile tight and pleased-seeming.

Look at that, Arthur thought. Now he became even more emboldened. "*Give* me those feet," he said, and lo and behold, she put her feet smack-dab in his lap. He rubbed them a little to warm her up, but then he stopped, because he was getting urges a guy had to be careful of. He started thinking about the algebra homework he had that night. Word problems, no less. That did it.

"I'm getting you all wet!" Nola said, and Arthur said, "Who cares?" She started to pull her feet away, and he grabbed her big toe. "This little piggy went to market," he said, and snorted, and she just about tipped right over, laughing. Just from that!

Well, she had no idea. He had a lot more than *that.*

"Oh, Frank!" she said. And then, realizing her mistake, she said, "I mean *Arthur*! I'm sorry. I meant Arthur."

"It's okay," Arthur said. But now his high spirits deflated. What a rollercoaster ride Nola was.

She put her feet back into the water.

"How is he?" She was staring straight ahead.

"Frank? He's all right."

She looked over at Arthur and sighed. "You know why I was crying?"

"Why?"

"Because I don't have a chance with your brother. It's just that he's so handsome and smart. And he seems like he's so much fun. Is he fun?"

"Yeah, I guess he is." *What about me?* Arthur thought.

"Let me ask you something," Nola said. "When Frank has a girlfriend, how long does it usually last?"

"I don't know. Depends, I guess. Like there was this one girl he liked for just week or so, Laura Johnson. Did you know her?"

"Didn't she move away?"

"Yeah, but he quit liking her before she moved away. That one was real quick."

"What's the longest he's liked someone? And, as he gets older, does it seem to last longer? He's about to graduate and—"

"Nola?" Arthur couldn't take it anymore. He had to do something. "Frank only likes blond girls."

Nola's face hardened.

"He told you that?"

"He didn't have to. That's all he ever picks. Blondes."

"Well, I have two words for him: Ava Gardner."

"Ho. Vivien *Leigh*," Arthur said.

Nola sniffed. "She might not be a natural brunette."

"Really?"

"Yes. I've seen pictures in movie magazines where she's blond."

"Well, I wouldn't know. But for my money, you can't beat a brunette. If I were picking, it would be brunettes every time."

Nola picked up a twig and began to peel bark from it. "I don't even really care. There are a lot of fish in the sea. In fact, I might have another interest already."

Was it him? Could it possibly be?

"My mom says sometimes something is right in front of you and you just don't see it until something *makes* you see it," she said.

Arthur's heart began to race. He picked up a rock and skipped it across the water. Six times. Not bad.

"Do you know Corky Daniels?" Nola asked. "The quarterback?"

Oh, no, Arthur thought. *No!* But he said, "Yes, I know who he is." A senior. Dark curly hair, tall, real wide shoulders.

"Well, maybe he'll be my next boyfriend. He's plenty interested in me. He asked me to the prom, but my parents won't let me go until I'm a junior. But I could pick him if I wanted to. There are some very nice things about him. I hadn't really paid much attention to him before this. But there are some nice things."

"I wouldn't pick him if I were you," Arthur said.

"Why not?"

"He's not very . . . discreet about girls." This was true.

Arthur had been in the bathroom at school one time when Corky was in there crowing about his conquests.

Nola crossed her arms. "Boys are so stupid."

". . . Yeah."

"I don't mean you, Arthur. I don't think of you as a boy. I mean, I know you're a boy, but I think of you as a friend. And I really appreciate all you tell me about other guys. You've got the inside scoop."

Above them, a crow leaned down and cawed in a way that almost sounded like a laugh. That bird was about right, Arthur thought. He said, "I'm not really very much like other guys, Nola."

"What do you mean?"

"For one thing, I'm not much interested in sports. I don't have many guy friends. I'm not . . . I don't know, *tough,* I guess, like I ought to be."

"Well, I think you're right on the beam."

Arthur smiled. "Thanks."

She tilted her head and regarded him. "And you know what? I'd say I kind of *depend* on you. For being so easy to talk to. And for feeling safe. It means a lot, Arthur. Nothing I tell you gets strange-seeming or taken the wrong way, or used against me. You know?"

He nodded. Impossible for him to say what he was thinking, which was *Isn't that love?*

Nola went on. "When I think of you, I think of someone who . . . well, this might sound odd, but you are someone who could tell me if I had something on my face and I wouldn't be embarrassed. You could even tell me my slip was showing."

He took in a breath and looked her right in the eyes. "I think of you sometimes at night, Nola."

She swallowed, and Arthur thought he saw a kind of nervousness come into her eyes.

She looked away and began speaking rapidly. "Isn't it funny, what can go through your head at night? The way thoughts stream in, one after the other, like a parade? And sometimes one thing has nothing to do with the other. But when I think of you . . ." She turned back to him, twin spots of pink on her cheeks. "Well, I guess what I mean to say, Arthur, is I just like you so much. I wish I could do something for you." She smiled and leaned forward, closer to him. "You want me to bake you a cake?"

"That would be great!"

Her smile faded. "Well, see? Now I have to tell you that I'm actually a terrible baker. Everything I try to bake burns. Every time. Another thing I'm just a big faker about."

"I wouldn't care if it were burned," he said.

She nodded. "You say that, but you would care."

"Oh, Nola, don't you see that—"

"Brrrr!" Shivering, she pulled her feet out of the water. She pulled her skirt down farther over her knees. Arthur saw that her feet were red, and she was hunched over herself, shivering.

"It's too early in the season to go wading, Nola."

"I know. But whenever spring comes, I just have to do it." Her teeth were chattering.

Arthur took off his jacket to wrap around her feet. That close to her, he could smell her perfume. He wanted so much to touch her cheek. How could he make it so that he might touch her cheek?

"You'll get your jacket all dirty," she said, pulling her feet away.

"I don't care."

"I do." She handed Arthur his jacket and looked around. "Where are my shoes?"

Arthur picked them up from where he'd put them, next to him. "Got 'em right here. I was guarding them."

She laughed. "You were *guarding* my *shoes*?"

"Yep."

"From what? Beavers?" She laughed again, harder.

Well, there were two ways to go here. He could be humiliated. Or he could tell her a story that would make Frank proud.

"It just so happens, Nola, that two beavers from this very park were recently arrested. Booked and charged."

"Is that right."

Nola's eyes had grown sparkly.

"What was the charge?" she asked.

"Use of saddle shoes in dam construction."

"I'll bet their mug shots were terrifying," she said.

"The profiles, especially. You know. Their teeth."

Nola said, "Well! I guess the moral of this story is that a girl shouldn't take her shoes off here."

"Not unless she's with the right guy."

She turned to look at him. Arthur stopped breathing. They were both so still. And then Nola looked at her watch. "Oh, my gosh! I have to go." She put her shoes on and stood up.

"I'll walk you home," Arthur said.

On the way, Nola told Arthur she wanted a lot of children someday, that she really liked kids—babies, especially. She said she had a way with babies. She told him she wished her name weren't Nola Corrine, she wished it were Marilyn Louise. She said her favorite flower was lilacs, and her favorite color was red. "Or blue. Maybe green." She fell silent, and Arthur wondered if it would be okay if he took her hand. But then she said, "Gosh. This town is so dull! When I graduate, I'm going to move to St. Louis and become an executive secretary. Or maybe . . . Oh, I can't even *think* of something to be!" She sighed. "You know when you said you aren't like other boys? At least you *know* that. You know who you *are*. I guess I don't." She pointed at the house they'd come to. "Oh well. We're here. Bye, Arthur."

He watched her climb the stairs, and then he remembered he had a five-dollar bill in his pocket from his work today. He'd forgotten he was rich.

Frank had once told him that if you were really serious about a girl, you should ask her out to dinner. He called it the old Number 49. Well, now Arthur could do it.

"Hey, Nola!" he called.

She turned around from where she'd been ready to open the door.

"Want to go out for supper tomorrow night?" One of his hands was squeezing the other to death.

"You mean . . . with you?"

"Yeah. I know it's a school night, but we can go early."

"Where?"

Good question. "It's a surprise."

Her face lit up. "That would be fun! But I have to go to my grandma's house for dinner tomorrow night. It's her birthday."

"How about Monday?"

"Cheerleading practice."

"Tuesday?"

"Play practice."

Arthur wasn't sure he should keep going, but he said, "Wednesday?"

"Student council."

"Oh. Okay, then." He got it. She didn't want to go. Humiliated, he started for home.

"Arthur?"

He turned around. "Yes?"

"I could go on Thursday. But I really would have to get home early."

"I'll pick you up at five o'clock. You'll be home by seven." His heart was like a kite: plummeting down one minute, soaring high the next.

"Wait there," Nola said. "I'll ask if I can go."

Arthur stood barely breathing on the sidewalk. Next door, a little girl came out of her house and started skipping rope. Then her little brother banged out the door, and the girl said, "Go back in! It's not your turn! I want to be alone!" He hoped that wasn't an omen.

But right after that, Nola stuck her head out the door and yelled, "We're on!"

Frank had once told Arthur that some writer fellow

said *summer afternoon* were the two most beautiful words in the English language. Not anymore.

Arthur walked down the sidewalk slowly, but what he wanted to do was bust out running. The little girl skipping rope stopped to watch him go by. Something must be showing, and he didn't care. A dinner date with Nola. Time to have a more serious conversation. He'd find a way to say the words he wanted to say to her. He was ready to remove any doubt about what he felt for her, to take the chance and put all his cards on the table. And he hoped he could finally see what *her* real feelings were. There had to be a way to ask her that. Even if what she said wasn't what he wanted to hear, at least he'd know.

After they were up in their room that night, he'd ask Frank where a fellow could bring a girl out for a dinner that wouldn't set him back too much. Arthur had a lot to discuss with Frank, in fact. But as it turned out, his brother was the one needing advice.

Chapter 15

WEDNESDAY EVENING, ARTHUR'S family had a cele-
bration dinner. His father had gotten the job, and
his mother had made beef stroganoff. Now they were fin-
ishing dessert, chocolate fudge cake served with vanilla ice
cream. Arthur's dad was acting strange—a little shy, but
also boastful. "You kids are going to reeeeeally like that
car I'm getting," he said. "Chevrolet Fleetmaster." He
said the name of the car like he was the one who'd thought
it up. He looked at Arthur's mother. "You'll like it too,
right?"

"Of course I will!" she said.

"I suppose we should sell Grimy," Arthur's father said,
and a long silence fell.

Finally, "Do we have to?" Arthur asked. There was
only one place Grimy would go, he figured, and that was
to the glue factory.

"Well, I don't need him or the cart anymore. I'll sell
that, too, if I can."

"He's our *horse,* Pop," Frank said.

Their father dragged some bread across his plate, then looked up at Frank. "It costs to feed him, son."

His tone was not unreasonable. Still, Frank and Arthur had had Grimy all their lives.

Frank leaned back his chair and crossed his arms. "I'll pay for his feed."

"I'll help, too," Arthur said.

"You don't make enough," their dad said to Arthur. To Frank, he said, "And you know we need a big part of your money for household expenses."

"I can still do that," Frank said. "But you'll be making a lot more money now, Pop."

"Maybe I will, but just . . . not right away. Let's just see how well I do." He was getting testy now.

"How about if we just wait awhile before we sell him?" Arthur's mother said. "We don't have to do it right away, do we, Eugene?"

"All right, you softies," their father said. "We'll keep him for as long as we can. But if I need to sell him, I'm going to sell him."

On Frank's face was written, *Over my dead body.* "I'm going upstairs," he said. "I have a lot of homework. Especially English." He looked at Arthur. *Oh.* He had something to tell him about Mary.

Arthur stood. "I got a lot, too."

"Go on, then," their dad said. He held up his empty dessert plate. "What are the chances of a fellow getting a second slice of heaven?" he asked.

"More coffee, too, sweetheart?" their mother answered, which made Arthur feel kind of sick. He didn't understand it. More than anything, he wanted his parents to be kind to each other, but this was not what he had in mind. This was like in the movies when somebody busted out singing to someone else and you just felt embarrassed for both of them.

When the brothers got to their room, Frank sat on the edge of his bed and shoved his hands between his knees. "Guess what."

"What."

"I talked to Mary today. It was a difficult conversation. I tried to be absolutely honest with her. I told her my biggest dream was to be a writer, and I didn't see how I could do it if I had a family to support. I could *try*—I could get a job and write maybe at night—but the truth is, most guys come home from work beat. If I worked all day, I'd have nothing left.

"I told her I didn't think we could go to New York now; it was just too complicated. Least if we stayed here, maybe Ma could help us out with the baby. I don't think either one of us would win any prizes for knowing how to take care of a baby. We weren't planning on that."

"How come she got pregnant, anyway, Frank? I mean, what happened?"

He shrugged. "The condom broke."

"Ah." Arthur nodded. Like *he* knew how that kind of thing could happen. He had learned the facts of life in a rudimentary way in health sciences class, but what he learned only raised more questions. You couldn't keep asking things; you'd look like a dope. Arthur had come very close to raising his hand and asking Mr. Sydlowsky, "Could you just explain how things fit together *exactly*?" But all those other guys in class, many of them leaning back in their desks with their arms crossed, snuck looks out the window, like all this was old hat to them. Instead of asking anything, Arthur leaned back and crossed his arms, too.

At some point he would understand everything, Frank had told Arthur, meaning to be reassuring, but all it did was make Arthur nervous. What if he didn't? All he knew about condoms, for example, was how they looked; Frank had unwrapped one once to show him. Arthur didn't like seeing it. It gave him a kind of squishy feeling: How in the world was a guy supposed to put *that* on?

"It was embarrassing when I told Mary all this," Frank said. "I felt like I was letting her down. But she was such a good sport about it. I was standing at the door to leave after we talked and I . . . Well, I cried. I was just so *sorry*, and so frustrated. And you know what she did? She pulled me over to sit down on the sofa and she took my face in her hands and she told me she loved me. She said she knew what we did was wrong. But she didn't want to compound it by taking my life from me. She said she could resign and go to a home for unwed mothers. Or, if I wanted, after I graduated, we could get married and try going to New York anyway. She could find a job somewhere, and I could write at least until the baby came. She's something, Arthur. She's really something."

"So what are you going to do?" Arthur asked. "Are you going to New York?"

Frank sighed. He looked so miserable.

"I don't see how I could write under the pressure of that kind of deadline. I just didn't think this through!"

"Then is she going to one of those homes?"

"I don't know, Arthur. I guess so."

This seemed like terrible news all around. He imagined a home for unwed mothers could be hard for Mary, and besides that, the dreadful substitute Miss Greely would no doubt take over her classes. What was the opposite of beautiful and kind Mary Anker? Miss hawk-nosed, beady-eyed Greely, who believed in paddling, using a board with holes drilled in it so it would hurt more. Who sent you to the principal's office if you so much as stared out the window. She got one kid suspended for passing gas, and it wasn't even on purpose that he did it.

"Did you tell her you loved her, at least?" Arthur asked Frank.

"Arthur. I *started* with that." He lay flat on his bed. "There's nothing worse than a woman being sweet to you when you're being terrible to her. I don't know what to do. And the baby growing inside, every day a little bigger." He looked over at Arthur. "Don't you ever get yourself in this kind of situation."

"I won't." For one thing, it would require a bit more knowledge than he possessed.

Quiet, and then Frank said, "So tell me how things are going with Nola."

Frank wanted to talk about something else, and Arthur was happy to oblige.

"Well, she sure talks about other guys a lot."

"In what way?"

"Like she tells me about guys she could pick to be her *boyfriend*. All these guys after her, all the time."

"You know what that is? Insecurity."

"What do you mean?"

"She doesn't think well of herself," Frank said. "She needs to build herself up by saying *so* many guys are after her. And, meanwhile, she probably doesn't care about a single one of them. Seems like she spends an awful lot of time with you, though."

"She *is* going out to supper with me tomorrow night."

"Shazam!"

"It's true."

"Where are you taking her?"

"I was hoping you'd have some suggestions. I've got five bucks."

"You could go to Whitey's Diner, over on Sycamore. You can get the hamburger steak dinner for a buck fifty. Girls like that place; it's really clean, and they have curtains on the windows, good music on the jukebox. Find out what she wants first. That's the polite thing to do, and also that way you'll know how much money you have left for what you want. And leave a nice tip; girls like that."

"Okay." Arthur felt scared, suddenly, thinking of him and Nola sitting in the restaurant. Just like guys always drove, they were supposed to take the lead in other things, too. What if he couldn't come up with what he wanted to say, or anything interesting at all? But even as he was worrying about it, he knew they could talk all day, he and Nola. They always had a good time talking, anyway.

"There's one big problem with Nola," Arthur said.

"What's that?"

"Seems like she just can't think of me as a boyfriend. She only likes me as a friend. She said she can rely on me; I'm so 'dependable.'"

"Oh, man," Frank said.

"I know."

"Kiss of death."

"Really?"

"Well, there's a way around that. You're going to have to do the old Number Seventeen. Make her jealous."

"Fat chance."

"You can do it."

"How?"

Frank laughed. "Even you can be that creative, Arthur. Make up something about another girl. Even better, ask another girl out and make sure Nola hears about it."

The creak of the stairs. Frank and Arthur grabbed schoolbooks and buried their noses in them.

The door opened and their father stuck his head in. "Everything going all right?"

"Yeah," Frank said.

"Okay, then."

He went back downstairs.

"He's acting so different," Arthur told Frank.

"I know. But I'm telling you, I just don't trust it."

"Do you think he was looking for us to say something to him?"

"Like what?"

"Like . . . I don't know, that we're proud of him?"

Frank thought about this. "The car is a pretty big deal," he said.

"That's what I mean. Maybe we should have asked him something about the car? Or told him that getting the job was great?"

"Maybe," Frank said. He looked over at Arthur. "Remember, Pop was an orphan. And he didn't get adopted until he was ten."

"Yeah, so?"

"So it makes a difference, Arthur. Pop's got a hole we won't ever fill."

Frank moved over to his desk and got busy with his homework. Arthur hadn't ever really thought of their dad that way, like a kid with a chink in him. *Unwanted.* Maybe that was why it had taken so long for Frank to fight back against him.

Arthur sat thinking, his chin in his hands. Scary people, gentle people, happy people, angry people, people who seemed like they didn't have a care in the world— they were all the same, in one respect. Inside them was a place that could get hurt so bad. Knowing that, it seemed like people would be more careful of one another. But people forgot. And Arthur, being a person, he forgot, too. He wished he could remember better. He thought it was like this: Inside everyone was a door that was meant to stay open, and it kept blowing shut. But every time you did something for someone else, why, that door opened again. And there was that little light.

Arthur was just about to start his own homework when he remembered that the next day was May 1. May Day! He had wanted to tie a bouquet on Nola's door. And now he knew what her favorites were: lilacs, which were blooming all over town.

"Frank?"

He looked up.

"I'm going to go out late tonight and steal some lilacs. Will you cover for me?"

"Steal lilacs? What for?"

"Tomorrow's May Day. Nola's favorite flower is lilacs. I want to put some on her porch so when she wakes up, there they'll be. Will you cover for me?"

"I'll help you get some. I know a place down by the tracks where there are tons of them. Just huge banks of lilacs."

"I'm not going down to the tracks at night."

"What are you going to do, take them from people's yards? You'll get caught. We'll go down to the tracks. Nothing will happen. We'll get her a gigantic bouquet. Forget those little nosegays you hang on the door. We'll take one of Grimy's pails and fill it with flowers. I'll put some water in one when I go out to bed him down and hide it in the bushes by the side of the house; it'll be all ready for us."

"Thanks, Frank."

"We'll get flowers for Mary, too. And Mom. Anyone else?"

"Grimy," Arthur said, laughing.

"Don't forget the chickens," Frank said, but he was deep into reading now.

Sometime after he had fallen asleep, Arthur heard Frank whispering his name. He woke up and looked at the clock: a little after one. "Let's go," Frank whispered.

They moved quietly in the darkness. Arthur followed Frank down the stairs, both of them carrying their shoes. Once they were outside, they put their shoes on and Arthur grabbed Grimy's pail. Then they set off, hunched over and walking slowly at first, then running. Halfway down the block, Mr. Adams's dog started barking like crazy, up on his hind legs at the window. They sped past, laughing, and before long they were going down a steep hill that led to the tracks; they had to hold on to the branches of bushes on the way down. They were way past the place where Arthur had met with the fortune teller; they were somewhere he'd never been, and Frank was right: here there were what seemed to be a million lilacs. Their scent was heavy in the air; it seemed to coat his throat. Arthur set the pail down.

"Give me the scissors," Frank said. "I'll get going on the ones way up on the top."

The scissors!

"I forgot them," Arthur said, shamefaced. Frank put his hands on his hips and shook his head.

"I've got a pen knife," Arthur said, and pulled it out of his pocket. It wasn't quite up to the job.

"We'll have to just break the branches," Frank said. "I don't know why you—" He stopped talking then and put his finger to his lips. In the woods nearby, there were men talking, what sounded like a large group of them, talking and laughing loudly. They were moving toward the brothers. Frank lowered himself down into the greenery and gestured for Arthur to do the same. They hid in the bushes until the sound faded.

"Who was that, do you think?" Arthur asked.

"Nobody."

"They sounded drunk."

"They were," Frank said.

"I don't know if we should stay here."

"Do you want to get Nola flowers?"

"Yeah, but—"

"Well, then, get going. Hurry up. Does she live far away?"

"Five or six blocks."

"We'll get them over there, then drop some off at Mary's and be home in less than an hour."

Arthur started breaking off branches. He was moving fast because he was afraid of those men coming back, but also because he was imagining Nola's face when she came out in the morning and found the biggest bouquet she'd ever seen. She might tell Arthur she'd never gotten anything like that in her life and start to see him in a whole different way.

After they'd loaded up Grimy's pail and Frank's arms, they headed over to Nola's house. When they arrived, Arthur used the twine Frank had brought along and tied together a number of branches to fashion a huge bouquet. Then he stood looking up at the second floor, wondering which window was Nola's bedroom, and how she looked sleeping. He wondered if she had lace on her nightgown, and then he wondered if she had rag rollers in her hair. If she did, she'd still be beautiful.

"Arthur!" he heard Frank whisper loudly, and he went as quickly and quietly as he could up the porch steps. He tied the bouquet to the door handle. He *had* remembered to bring the piece of paper with NOLA written on it, and he stuck that right at the top. He'd made the writing pretty fancy, with a decorative line drawn under her name. He didn't sign his name. *Girls like surprises.* He'd tell her at dinner that he had been the one.

He stood back and looked at the flowers. Nola might do a cheerleader jump split when she saw this bouquet. She was not captain of her cheerleading squad, but she jumped the highest. And she was the prettiest. You put a red ribbon in blond hair, that was nice. You put a red ribbon in black hair and you could die.

"Arthur!" Frank whispered again, and jerked his thumb toward the road: *Let's go!*

When they brought lilacs to Mary's house, Frank stuck them in her mailbox with a note he pulled from his pocket.

Arthur thought it would probably make Mary swoon. There were definite advantages to being a writer when it came to situations like this.

When they got home, they tied the last of the lilacs to the front door. Their mother would find them in the morning when she went out for the paper. Arthur was happy they'd done that for her. He guessed that when you were in love, it made you think of ways to love other people, too.

Chapter 16

THURSDAY AFTERNOON, AFTER school, Arthur was alone in the house. He paced in his bedroom, back and forth, looked out the window, sat on his bed, got up and paced again. What had Nola thought when she got the lilacs? And why was it that now, when he'd finally gotten a date with her, he was more unhappy than before?

Although *unhappy* wasn't really the right word, he supposed. He was just nervous, and he'd have to wait for over an hour before he could go to pick Nola up. It was awful; he couldn't stop thinking about what he might do wrong. This wouldn't be the casual kind of encounter they'd had so far. This was a *date*. A lot was riding on it. He went to the bookcase for a collection of riddles he'd given Frank a few years ago; surely a joke would be a good icebreaker for after they sat down together, but the book was nowhere to be found.

His suddenly lovey-dovey parents had gone out for a

ride in the country in his father's new car. Frank had gone to be with Mary. What Arthur needed was a friend. Never mind that everyone liked Arthur; he didn't really have someone he could call up or spontaneously visit. Frank had filled the role of brother and friend all of Arthur's life, and now he began to wonder if he'd relied on his brother for too much. Soon Frank would be off to New York, and then where would Arthur be? Playing cards with Grimy? It occurred to Arthur that the first step in getting a friend was admitting you needed one.

He went downstairs and began pacing in the living room. Then, deciding he had to get out of the house, he went to the telephone and pulled out the directory. Only one Guldorp was listed, and Arthur sat on the little telephone bench and dialed.

A woman answered.

"Hello, Mrs. Guldorp, this is Arthur Moses, calling for Harvey?" he said.

"Who?"

"Arthur Moses?"

Silence.

"I'm a friend of Harvey's from school? I came over not long ago?"

"*Arthur,* you say? And you're a friend from—" She stopped speaking to address someone in the background. Her voice was muffled from having put her hand over the receiver, but Arthur heard, "Well, *fine,* then! *Here!*"

Harvey's adenoidal voice came on the line. "Arthur?"

"Yeah, it's me. What are you doing?"

"Nothing."

"Want me to come over?"

"What for?"

Arthur sighed. "I don't know. We could read some comics."

"Well, I *did* just get some new ones. Dick Tracy, Felix the Cat, Superman, and a few others. I'm done with the Superman ones. You want to read those?"

"Sure. I'll come right over. Maybe we can do some other stuff, too." In truth, Arthur had no earthly idea what else to suggest. A guy suffered from not being much interested in or talented at sports. He supposed it was good Harvey was the same way. At least going to see him would pass an hour. If Arthur stayed home, he'd wear the carpets out with his pacing.

Outside, the day was fine, and Arthur felt immediately better. Amazing what could happen when the sky became your roof. The trees had all leafed out, the flowers were pushing up from their beds. Arthur picked up his pace.

When he got to Harvey's, Arthur rang the bell and Harvey answered the door in his stocking feet. "Come on up," he said, and now there was an enthusiasm and warmth in his voice that made Arthur glad he had called.

Harvey's room was nothing like Arthur had imagined it would be. It was warm and cheerful. There was a big window that let in a lot of light, a bed with a blue chenille spread, a pine dresser with models of cars displayed along the top. On a small desk with a gooseneck lamp, school-books were piled neatly off to the side. Arthur found himself glad to be here.

They settled themselves on the floor with their backs

against Harvey's bed, a stack of comics between them. Arthur noticed an Archie comic book and pulled it out of the pile.

"Who do you like better," Harvey asked, "Betty or Veronica?"

"Veronica," Arthur said.

"Betty," said Harvey. He turned to his Dick Tracy comic.

"Why Betty?" Arthur asked, thinking Harvey would say it was because she was blond. But he was wrong, because Harvey said, "She's nice. Veronica is too much trouble."

Arthur thought about this. "Sometimes a girl is *worth* a lot of trouble."

Harvey made no comment, which made for a relaxed feeling in Arthur. Maybe here was a place to experiment with things. And a way, apparently, to be honest, because when Harvey finally asked him about why some girls were worth it, Arthur answered readily, telling him a little about Nola, including the fact that he was taking her out for dinner tonight. "I might be in love," he said. It just burst out of him.

Harvey nodded gravely. "Yeah, it happens. I knew something was up with you, Moses. Hanging around after school every day the way you do. I knew it was some girl. I didn't know it was Nola McCollum, though. *Nobody* can have *her*. Want some free advice? You shouldn't waste your time that way, hanging around after school. Girls don't respect guys who do things like that. Tell you one thing, the Green Hornet would never wait around after school for some girl to come out. He would just suck her in with his quiet masculinity. That's what I do."

Arthur tried not to laugh out loud. "Have you got a girlfriend?" he asked.

Harvey put down his comic book. "Name of Patty Simpson ring a bell?"

"Really?" Patty was just a freshman, but she was cute as could be. Real short; shiny dark hair cut into a bob. Friendly, one of those who greeted every person she passed in the hall.

"Really," Harvey said.

"I didn't know that," Arthur said. "Congratulations." *Congratulations???*

But Harvey just said, "Thanks." He waved his comic book like a fan in front of his face. "Hot in here. Want to go outside?"

"I don't have much time left," Arthur said.

"That's okay," Harvey said. "We'll just take a little walk." He pointed to the downstairs and whispered, "She eavesdrops sometimes."

When they got outside, Harvey confided that he had kissed Patty Simpson three times. Arthur nodded, impressed.

"Have you kissed Nola yet?" Harvey asked.

"Nope," Arthur said.

"Have you kissed any girl?"

"Not really."

"Well, it's actually pretty easy," Harvey said. "And they

usually like it. Just remember to go slow or they can get jumpy."

"Okay," Arthur said. "Do you shut your eyes?"

"You can," Harvey said. "Either way."

They took a short walk to the end of the block and back, talking effortlessly. It seemed they both liked catching tadpoles and releasing them. They both liked walking deep into the woods, and Harvey had plans to buy a tent so that he could sleep out there.

Then it was time for Arthur to go.

"Try to relax," Harvey said. "Think of it this way. Nola has something you want; alls you have to do is come up with something *she* wants. You've got to realize you have a lot to offer. You're so much better than those lunkheads she hangs around with."

For a few minutes after he waved goodbye to Harvey and started for Nola's house, Arthur was convinced that Nola was the lucky one. That feeling didn't last long. But he'd had it.

Chapter 17

ARTHUR CLIMBED THE steps to Nola's house, rang the bell, and then took a couple of steps back to wait. His breathing felt constricted; it was as though his belt had migrated up from his waist to cinch around his chest. Nola's father answered the door. He was a tall man, dressed in black pants and a white shirt open at the collar, the sleeves rolled up. He had glasses at the end of his nose and held a folded newspaper in one hand. "Arthur Moses?" he bellowed, but it was a friendly sound.

Arthur managed a "Yes, sir."

He opened the door wider. "Well, come on in! Meet the family!"

Arthur came into the living room and stood there, trying to remember to keep his hands out of his pockets. Nola's mom came out from the kitchen, wiping her hands on her apron. "Well, *hi* there!"

They certainly were friendly! Arthur relaxed a little. "Hi," he said, smiling. "I'm Arthur Moses."

Nola's mother walked up very close to him. It was almost as though she had trouble seeing, she was so close. "It's very nice to meet you," she said. "Nola will be right down. You two are going out to *dinner*, is that right?"

"Yes, ma'am."

"So fancy! And on your first date!"

Mr. McCollum came over and put his arm around his wife's shoulder. "You remember where I took you on our first date?"

"I certainly do," she said. "Ice-skating! And all I did was fall down."

"And all I did was pick you up," Mr. McCollum said. "And I couldn't have been happier."

"You know where he took me afterward, Arthur? Out for ice cream! When I was just freezing!"

"I guess I should have offered her hot chocolate," Mr. McCollum said. He looked at his wife. "But things worked out."

A boy around ten years old walked into the room. He was wearing belted denim pants and a Roy Rogers T-shirt. He stared at Arthur.

"Hello," Arthur said. "I'm Arthur Moses."

"I know."

Mrs. McCollum turned to her son. "Well, for heaven's sake, Timothy, introduce yourself! This is Nola's *date* for the evening."

This wasn't just Nola's date for the evening, Arthur was thinking. This was Nola's first date with him like it was Mr. and Mrs. McCollum's first date all those years ago. This was the beginning of the inevitable. (Another suggestion from Harvey, for how to think about this night. Also from Harvey: Project *confidence*. And take long strides.)

But Timothy, standing there and staring at him, was starting to get on Arthur's nerves.

"Do you play any sports?" Timothy asked.

"Nope." Arthur raised his eyebrows and tried to look friendly.

"Nothing?"

Before he could answer, here came Nola clattering down the stairs. "Hi, Arthur!" she said. "Ready?"

Was he ever.

Leave it to Frank. Whitey's Diner was the perfect place. It had a good, homey smell, like bread in the oven. There were some luscious-looking pieces of chocolate and coconut cake and all kinds of pie in the display case. There were some grown-ups there, but there were teenagers, too. Arthur and Nola got a booth right away and they sat down and folded their hands on the table. Arthur, after careful deliberation, had dressed in a white shirt and an argyle sweater vest, navy-blue dress pants, and his good shoes. Before he'd left to go to Mary's, Frank had lent him a tie, and even knotted it for him. He'd told Arthur to lay off the cologne. Or if he wanted to wear a *little*, okay, but don't take a bath in it. He'd grabbed a few dollars from his dresser drawer and shoved them into Arthur's pocket. Just in case, he'd said. Arthur had protested, and Frank said he could pay him back. Better to have a little extra, he said; you never know. You didn't want to come up short on cash on a first date.

Arthur thought he looked fine. But Nola! She was wearing a creamy-white blouse with billowy sleeves that made her look like an angel dropped down to earth. There was a silky black bow tied at her neckline. She wore little pearl earrings and a charm bracelet. She had on a black-and-white patterned skirt that looked like it was just dying for a fellow to spin her around in it, and he wished he could. She had on nylon stockings and pretty black shoes with straps that crossed over each other. And she was wearing red lipstick.

There was a jukebox in the corner and "That's My Desire" was playing. It said things Arthur hardly dared to think, and he was afraid the tips of his ears would redden if he paid too much attention, so right away he started talking. "Looks good, huh?" he asked, referring to the menu the waitress had given them when she put down dinner rolls and water. He quickly scanned the prices and said, "Get what*ever* you want."

Nola could get the fanciest thing on the menu: the Spencer steak that came with french fries and hearts of lettuce was $1.40. They could both have it, and he'd still have plenty left over for them each to have dessert.

"I guess I'll have the combination plate," Nola said. That was just a hamburger and french fries. "And maybe the vanilla malt?"

"You're sure that's all?" Arthur asked.

Nola pointed to the desserts on the counter. "I might be saving room for some pie. They all look scrumptious."

"I'll order the exact same thing," Arthur said.

When the waitress came over, he ordered for Nola first and then for himself, as Frank had told him to do. Then he and Nola sat waiting. Arthur could not think of one blessed thing to say. "Too Fat Polka" was playing on the jukebox now, and he didn't think it would be polite to talk about that. He was dying to hear what she thought about the lilacs, but he decided to wait awhile. He didn't want to be one of those people who give a gift and then hang all over the recipient, saying, "Do you like it?"

Nola was saying something.

"Pardon?" Arthur asked.

"I was asking if you had any hobbies?" Her voice was different—a little breathy—and Arthur wondered if she was nervous, too.

"I guess a few," he said.

"What are you most passionate about?"

You.

"Well, I like to put together models."

"Uh-huh." She didn't seem exactly knocked out. He wasn't going to tell her he liked stamps, although he did. A kid from school named Sheldon Mitchell regularly brought in stamps to show Arthur at lunchtime; he was a collector. Arthur liked the pictures on a lot of those stamps, and Sheldon told him about the history some of the images represented. He and Arthur sat at the same

table in the cafeteria. It was one of those random-kid ta-
bles where those who didn't have a group sat. In addition
to Sheldon and Arthur there was a girl named Emily Beek-
man who always sat at their table. She talked really loud
and often what she said didn't make much sense. Arthur
tried to defend her sometimes, but a guy didn't want to
stick his neck out too far. Nola sat with the popular girls,
next to the jock table.

So, no, Arthur didn't want to mention stamps. He
wanted to have a nice, easy conversation that might let
him segue into what he *really* wanted to say.

"I guess you might say my favorite hobby is trees," he
said, then instantly regretted it. He had to stop himself
from smacking his forehead.

But Nola's eyes brightened. "Really?"

"Yup. They're very interesting."

The waitress brought their platters over and put them
down.

Nola put a french fry in her mouth and smiled at Arthur. Out of his labor, he was feeding her. He felt like Tar-
zan.

"Tell me something about trees," Nola said. She
seemed more relaxed now.

"I like their names, for one thing. Eastern redbud. Sycamore. Cottonwood. Black locust."

"Tell me something about the redbud tree."

Arthur took a bite of his hamburger and thought for a
minute. "Well, it's one of the earliest trees to bloom every
spring. If you look at the tree when it's young, the branches

look like a vase. The blossoms are usually a pinkish purple, but right down my block is a bush with white flowers.
And guess what? You can eat those flowers, raw or
cooked."

Nola's eyes widened. "You can?"

"Yup."

"Did you ever do that?"

"Nope."

"Did you ever want to?"

Arthur shrugged. "Not alone."

"Should we do it sometime? I'd try it."

"Sure!"

Arthur was happy. He was so happy.

The door burst open and Corky Daniels came in, followed by three guys on the football team. The rest of the
guys sat down in a booth, but Corky made a beeline
toward Arthur's table: he'd seen Nola.

"Hey, good-looking," he said, giving her one of those
suave looks Arthur would never even attempt. To Arthur:
"Hey, Moses." Back to Nola: "Did you get my May Day
card?"

She smiled. "Yessss, and I also got your *bouquet*. I have
never seen a bouquet of lilacs so big in all my life!"

Corky hesitated, then said, "That right?"

"Yes, thank you so much, Corky. That was the sweetest
thing. I divided them up and there are lilacs in every room
in my house. I was going to write you a thank-you note,
but here you are, so . . . thank you!"

"Yeah! You're welcome."

Arthur was like a mannequin, frozen in place.

Nola pointed to her plate. "Better get back to this before it gets cold," she said to Corky.

"Sure. We'll talk later."

He walked back over to the booth and said something to the rest of the guys, who erupted in laughter.

"He's nothing," Nola said quietly.

It occurred to Arthur to tell her right then and there that it wasn't Corky who'd brought her those lilacs. But he worried that it would be awkward; it might make Nola feel foolish that she had assumed it.

Besides, he had more things he wanted to tell Nola about the redbud, things that Corky wouldn't know about in a million years. He wanted to start by saying that its leaves were heart-shaped and let that hang in the air. (Frank: *Leave a little mystery.*) Then he'd say that the redbud was called an understory, because it could grow in the shade of taller trees. "A feisty little tree, don't you agree?" he would say, maybe leaning toward her. "Determined. Stronger than you might think."

But then Nola said, "I was just thinking. You know those names of trees you told me?"

"Yeah?"

She slurped a bit of her malt and regarded him from over the rim of the glass. "They sound like a jump-rope rhyme:

> *"Eastern redbud, sycamore tree*
> *Who's the fellow that's meant for me?"*

Arthur stared at her.

"Lots of jump-rope rhymes are like that," Nola said. "About love and who your husband will be."

He swallowed. "Is that right?"

Tex Williams came on the jukebox: *Smoke, smoke, smoke that cigarette!*

Nola's face lit up and she sang along. There went the mood.

They talked a little more and ended up sharing a piece of butterscotch pie, which Arthur thought could have been romantic if it hadn't been for Corky coming back over and leaning on the table like he owned it. "Looks *good*," he said, looking right at Nola. Nola picked up her water glass and kept drinking, saying nothing until he left.

"Nola?"

"Yes?"

"It wasn't Corky who brought you those lilacs."

She was confused. "What do you mean?"

"He just said that. I brought them to you. My brother and I went out and cut them late at night and brought them over."

"Oh, my goodness!" Nola said.

Arthur told her all about his and Frank's escapade and she listened, wide-eyed. When he'd finished, she said, "You and *Frank* did that for me?"

"Yes."

She looked over at Corky, then back at Arthur. "Gosh. Thank you."

"You're welcome."

Was this the time? Should he say "I got them for you because I'm crazy about you"? He took in a breath, but Nola was picking up her purse. "This was so much fun, Arthur, but I have to get home."

"Right," he said. The Nola Shuffle: two steps forward, one step back. He was full of despair. This was the night he was going to make Nola see how much he cared, and to see if she cared, too. But he sure hadn't gotten very far. Frank could advise him all he liked, but Arthur didn't have the same gift for language that his brother did. Arthur was tired of trying to think of things to say that would get him somewhere with Nola; he just wanted to *be* there, past all effort, beyond all doubt.

She stood, he stood, and they walked together to the cash register. In the case were gifts you might want to buy on your way out. Nola bent over to examine the spaghetti poodle with puppies on chains. "Look!" she said. "Isn't that cute? Look how one of the puppies is pink!"

"Uh-huh," Arthur said.

"And look at the carpet coin purses!" Nola said. "That one with the flowers? Why, if you used it, it would be like getting a bouquet every day. But the one with the cat is just too adorable."

"Which of those things do you like best?" Arthur asked.

Nola looked at the poodles, then back and forth at the coin purses. Finally, she pointed.

"The cat coin purse," she said. "It's the cutest. Look at his little paws, tucked up so tight against him. I wish I could have a cat, but I can't, because my father is allergic.

But when I have my own place, I'm always going to have cats, and I'm always going to name them Gordon."

Arthur chuckled.

Nola turned quickly to him. "Do you think that's a silly name for a cat?"

"Absolutely not!" said Arthur. "I'm laughing because it's so perfect!"

The cashier came to the register, and Arthur dug in his pocket for his wallet.

"I'm just going to powder my nose," Nola said, and Arthur nodded. He paid the bill and then asked how much for the coin purse. With the money Frank had given him, he had enough.

He remembered when Nola had told him she wished she had a different name, and on a paper napkin, he wrote:

For Nola, who should never change her name.
Or anything else about herself. From your friend,
Arthur.

He felt a little bad writing *friend,* but what else was he to her? He put the note in the purse, asked the cashier to put it in a bag, and quickly hid it in his jacket pocket; Nola had come out of the ladies' room and was walking toward him.

As they started on their way to Nola's house, she said, "Arthur? Do you know anything else about that tree? The redbud?"

"Sure. One thing is you can make a tea from the yellow dye in the twigs. It can cure headaches and muscle pain."

"Gosh. Seems like you know all kinds of things other people don't."

"I don't know about that. I just think when you like something so much, you naturally want to find out more about it. For instance, I'd like to know a lot more about *you*."

"You would?" Nola smiled and said, "Well, I wouldn't tell anyone else this, but . . ."

"What?" Arthur asked.

"Okay, there's this one tree? And every time I pass it, I think it looks like it's saying 'Harumph!' I guess that sounds crazy, but—"

"The one on Green Street? Great big tree in the middle of the block where the trunk kind of looks like it's sticking its chest out all snooty?"

Nola's eyes widened. "Yes! You know it, then!"

"Sure," Arthur said, trying to hide his pride.

"Well, gosh! I just think it's kind of *wonderful* that we both can see that. Don't you?"

Yes! Yes! Yes! Arthur thought, but he answered with a casual "Mm-hmm."

Nola stopped walking. They were at her house. They stood there for a minute, saying nothing, and then Arthur held out the bag with the purse inside it. "This is for you."

"Leftovers?"

"Nope. Look inside."

She opened the bag and squealed. "The cat coin purse! Thank you!"

"Happy May Day," Arthur said.

She held the purse up close to her chest. "I'm keeping this forever!" She kissed his cheek and ran up on her porch.

Before she opened the door to go inside, she turned around to say, "And thank you for those beautiful lilacs! That Corky is such a liar!"

He imagined Nola opening the purse and finding the note he'd written to her. He saw her standing there in her bedroom and reading it with a little smile on her face. Maybe she'd keep it on her dresser and look at it every day. He knew she'd like it, anyway. "The advantage you have over the jocks is that you have a functioning brain in your head," Harvey had told him. "And you can be creative. Jocks are like cavemen. 'Me want woman. Me club on head and drag 'way.'"

It might be true, Arthur thought. A mystery, then, why so many girls went for jocks. Nola had said Corky was nothing. But she had looked at him in a way that worried Arthur. Not flirtatiously, perhaps, but not *not* flirtatiously.

It was over now, their date. And Arthur realized he didn't know how to feel about it.

Chapter 18

ARTHUR WAS HELPING Mrs. Crawford put in a variety of rose that was so dark purple it looked black. He'd never seen anything like it. After they'd settled the roots into the ground, he stood looking at it and suddenly got sad.

"Arthur?" Mrs. Crawford said.

It all came spilling out: How Arthur was trying to start something special with Nola and just couldn't seem to make any real progress. She was all he thought about. But so many boys were after her. He told Mrs. Crawford about how he and Frank had brought Nola a huge bouquet of lilacs in the middle of the night and then Corky Daniels had taken credit for it.

"But didn't you tell her it was you who brought the flowers?" Mrs. Crawford asked.

"I did, but . . ." He shrugged. "Those kind of guys just seem to have the advantage no matter what."

Mrs. Crawford leaned on her shovel. "If you won't tell

anyone about my bad language, I'll tell you something about Corky Daniels."

"Okay," Arthur said.

"He's a little shit."

Arthur felt himself flushing.

"Well, he *is*. His family goes to our church, and you should see how he sits there, so full of himself, as though he's waiting for admirers to come and kiss his hand. He's rude to everyone, including his parents. If he were my son, I'd get after him with the licking stick."

Mrs. Crawford didn't have any children. She had once told Arthur that she felt he was almost like a son to her. He could see that she felt bad for him now.

"Finish patting down the soil and give the bushes a good drink," Mrs. Crawford said. "And then why don't you come inside for some lemonade?"

After Arthur finished working, he climbed the steps to the back door. He wiped his feet on the mat, rubbed his dirty hands on his pants, pushed down on his cowlick, and knocked.

"I'm in the dining room," he heard her call. "You can wash up at the kitchen sink and then come on back."

Arthur had never been in Mrs. Crawford's house before. The dining room was something to behold; the pretty carpet with colors like scattered jewels, the polished silverware next to the places she had set, the portraits on the wall. One was a serious-faced, mustachioed man, and one was of Mrs. Crawford in a blue evening gown that Arthur only glimpsed but wished he could stare at forever.

Arthur sat down at the table and Mrs. Crawford poured

him some lemonade. He drank from a glass with initials etched into the side. There was a big bouquet of roses in the center of the table, white ones that had a little green eye at the center. This was how some people lived!

He thought of his own house: the stained upholstered living room chairs with scratches on the wooden arms, the old-model radio in the corner, the braided rug that was coming undone here and there, the reading lamp that required your pulling on the chain just so or it wouldn't go on. The framed pictures on the wall had come from calendars. The magazines his mother fanned out on the coffee table were hand-me-downs from Mrs. Munson, who lived next door. The big flowers on the living room drapes had faded into a color that wasn't a color at all. In the kitchen, the yellowing linoleum was lifting in one corner, and a piece of matchbook kept one kitchen chair from wobbling. Their white-enamel roaster had big chips, and the cord on the toaster was fraying. The dining room was still nice, and his mother labored to keep the table shiny, but seeing Mrs. Crawford's furniture made Arthur understand that his family's was of an inferior quality. Still, he loved seeing the twin beds in his parents' room, even if the bedspreads weren't satin like in the magazines but rather burgundy chenille, and he knew his mother took great pride in the sweet potato plant on the nightstand that she'd started years ago and was still flourishing. And he especially loved the bedroom he shared with Frank: their beds and desks, the high little windows, the radiator that hissed and occasionally boiled over but kept them so warm in the winter.

Mrs. Crawford sat down at the table opposite Arthur. "Nola McCollum," she said.

At first Arthur thought she was telling him the name of the roses on the table. Mrs. Crawford was always telling him the names of her rosebushes, so many different names that he had trouble keeping track of them all. Madame Hardy, Queen of Sweden—you never knew what a rose might be called. It was pretty interesting that people sat around thinking of names for flowers and trees . . . But then Arthur realized Mrs. Crawford was talking about *his* Nola.

He hoped Mrs. Crawford wasn't going to say anything bad about her, and she didn't. She said, "Such a sweet and lively girl. And just as pretty as she can be."

"I love her," Arthur blurted out, and then was overcome with embarrassment. He snuck a look at Mrs. Crawford to see if she was smiling one of those grown-up smiles that was like a pat on top of your head. But she wasn't. She looked dead serious.

"Let me tell you something, Arthur. People go a long way to try to discredit the notion of love in people who they think are too young to have such emotions. I don't feel that way at all. I loved someone when I was your same age, and you know what?"

"You married him?" Arthur asked, in a near whisper.

She smiled. "No. I didn't. As it happened, he . . . well, he married someone else. And I married my husband, and I'm not a bit sorry that I did. But I think of that young man so often—Eddie Franklin was his name—and I don't doubt for a minute that what I felt for him was love, pure and simple. I guess in a way, I'll always love him."

"But you love your husband, too, right?" Arthur asked, and then immediately regretted it. For one thing, he didn't want to think that if you loved someone as much as he loved Nola, you could just go on and love someone else, like you were changing your mind about what color socks to wear. He didn't want to love anyone but Nola, ever. In addition to that, this was a very personal question. But Mrs. Crawford answered right away.

"I do love my husband. And now that he's . . . Can I tell you something confidential, Arthur? And trust that you'll keep it to yourself?"

Arthur sat up straighter. "Yes, ma'am."

"My husband is ill."

"Oh! I'm sorry."

"Thank you. We're not sure what's going to happen; right now we're very hopeful about a doctor in Minnesota who treated him. His illness has made me realize how very much I love him. But it's a different love from what I felt for Eddie. There's nothing like first love. It's a kind of . . . *fury*, isn't it?"

Arthur thought that was exactly the right word to put on a feeling that had you in a powerful grip, one that made you soar but also devastated you, sometimes at the same time.

"I don't think you have anything to worry about with Corky Daniels," Mrs. Crawford said.

That made Arthur feel a little better, but Nola had already said that Corky was out of the running, anyway. Not all the guys she talked about were little shits.

Mrs. Crawford reached across the table to refill Arthur's glass. She said, "You know, Arthur, sometimes it takes a girl a while to come to appreciate someone like you. You're different from most other boys."

"I know," he said miserably. Frank was a doer, the kind of guy who, if he was in comic books, would have all kinds of POW!!s around him. Arthur was more of a watcher. When he was alone, he didn't mind it. But when he was with others, he often wished he could be more like them.

But now Mrs. Crawford said, "Being different is a wonderful thing. Nola will come to see it. In fact, based on what you've told me, she already has. For a girl to feel she can say things to a boy—personal things—to feel that she can be honest, that means a lot. You have so much integrity, Arthur, so much reliability. I have a feeling she'll come to treasure that. And then I'll have to give you bouquets for two!"

Now Arthur couldn't help smiling.

"Ready to get back out there and work some more?"

He wasn't sure if she was talking about the garden or Nola. But in any case, the answer was yes. He stood up. "Mrs. Crawford? I just want to say I'm awful sorry about your husband, and I hope he gets better soon."

"I hope so, too. Thank you, Arthur. Now, let's get out in the sunshine and dig our cares away. If you can't find solace in nature, there's no solace to be found."

Later, before Arthur left, Mrs. Crawford cut him a

bouquet of pink roses. "Your mother will love these," she said. "They last a long time."

On the way home, Arthur spied Frank coming down the sidewalk. He hadn't seen Arthur yet; his head was hanging low, his hands in his pockets. But just before he reached Arthur, he looked up.

"Hey!" he said, grinning. "Where are you going?"

"Home," Arthur said.

"Come with me, why don't you?"

"Well . . ." Arthur looked at the bouquet.

"Okay, let's go and give them to Ma, and then you want to come with me?"

"Where are you going?"

"Reconnaissance."

Arthur liked the sound of that. "Sir, yes, sir!" he said, and Frank cuffed the back of his head.

"That's for nothing," Frank said. He was in a good mood now.

They gave their mother the flowers and she was her usual appreciative self. She thanked Arthur and kissed him and ran off to the dining room for her crystal vase.

"We're going out," Frank called after her. "Okay?"

They could barely hear her response, but they knew she'd said some version of *okay*. She was busy making dinner. Weekends had become more special because of their dad being gone all week. He wasn't making much money yet, but he was doing okay. It had been much better at home these days, though Frank and Arthur were still wary of believing things had changed for good.

They walked for a while, and when they were just outside of downtown, Frank's mood seemed to change; he looked serious. "Bowl of chili at Birdie's?" he asked Arthur.

"Okay by me."

They sat at one of the rickety wooden booths by the window that had initials carved all over the tabletop. With some trepidation, he looked for N.M. Nope, not yet. Someday he would carve A.M. + N.M.

After lunch was delivered, Frank said, "All right. I came to a decision. And I'm not going back on it. I'm driving myself crazy going back and forth when the truth about what I should do is obvious."

"You're going to marry her and move to New York."

"Is that what you think I decided?"

Arthur sighed. "Yep." The chili wasn't so good anymore. He put down his spoon.

"Wrong. I am going to marry her, but I'm not going anywhere."

Arthur's mouth fell open. "Honest?"

"Honest." He leaned forward and asked, "Where can a writer work?"

"I don't know. Anywhere, I guess."

"Exactly. So that's what I'm going to do. I'm going to marry her, move into her house with her, and finish school. She won't be showing much until July or so, so she can finish out the school year herself. Then I'll support her with some job I get. I'll write early in the morning or late at night. Lots of writers have done that. Once I sell a book, why, then we'll move to New York."

"Sounds like a good plan," Arthur said. "But you might decide you want to stay here."

"Nope."

"Good place to raise a kid."

"Arthur. *No*."

"Suit yourself." Arthur's feelings were a little hurt, but then he reasoned that they shouldn't be. The truth was that Frank would simply never feel about Mason the way that Arthur did. Maybe the way to look at this was that it could be great, Frank living in New York. He would surely come back to visit Mason, and Arthur could visit him in the big city. He could take the train. It could be exciting. Maybe Nola would come with him. They'd be a little older. Nola would be wearing white gloves and he would be wearing a hat and he would carry her luggage.

"So," Frank said, "my mission today is to get a ring."

"An engagement ring?"

Frank nodded.

"You mean a *diamond*?"

"Yup."

Arthur blew some air out of his cheeks. "That's a lot of dough."

"Don't I know it. But I've been working a lot, and I think I've got enough, even with contributing to the family the way I have been. It's the right thing to do, Arthur. Why should she have to bear the burden of going through this alone? We got into this together. A baby came along too soon, but we can make do. We'll be all right. The main thing is, I love her. That comes before everything. I *love* her. You know, after the tornado, I went over to see if she was all right. And when I saw her little house still standing there, and she came out on the porch, I just about . . . We *ran* to each other. And we didn't say a word, but I'm sure we were both thinking the same thing, which was *As long as there's you*. Do you know what I mean, Arthur?"

Did he ever. "I sure do," he said.

After Frank paid for lunch, the brothers went to Hermann's Jewelers. Arthur got the willies walking in there; it seemed like they'd have to pay just to breathe the air. It was quiet as a library. The thick carpet was royal blue. There was a crystal chandelier hanging from the ceiling. The cases were full of shiny, glittery things: watches, necklaces, bracelets. And in the back was a whole case just for wedding rings. There was a stand-up cardboard picture on top of that case showing a woman smiling all giddy, holding up her hand with an engagement ring on it. DIAMONDS ARE FOREVER, the sign said.

Arthur felt like they should turn around, but Frank was all confidence now. "Like to see some engagement rings," he said in a breezy way to the man behind the front counter.

"Very good," the man said. He was wearing a light-blue suit with a pocket handkerchief and shoes you could probably see yourself in. "Right over here," he said, moving to stand behind the case in the rear of the store. He held out his hand to Frank. "Bill Runk," he said.

Frank told him his name and then bent down to see the rings better.

"Wowser," he said quietly.

"Any price in mind?" the guy asked.

"Well, I guess maybe I'd like to just look for a minute and find one I like and then we can see how much it is. How's that?"

"You bet. Take your time," Bill said, and went off to help a woman who'd just come into the store.

"I think I might be in trouble," Frank whispered to Arthur.

"Why?"

He pointed at the rings. "The price tags are all turned over. That means they cost a lot."

"Don't know unless you ask. You'll find one."

Frank looked over at him. "That's the spirit," he said, and kept on looking.

By the time Bill came back, Frank had settled on two choices. One Arthur had suggested, and he felt proud that Frank was considering it.

Bill slid behind the case again and asked Frank, "So? Anything appeal?"

"Two," Frank said, and pointed. "Can I see that one first?"

Bill pulled out a black velvet pad and laid it down on the countertop, then placed the ring with the bigger stone on top of it.

"Very nice choice," he said to Frank. "Clarity and cut are both excellent."

It was a big diamond in a simple setting. But when the man showed Frank the price, it was clearly too much.

Arthur moved closer to his brother. "You know, seeing it close up, I don't like it as much," he said.

"I agree," Frank said, though Arthur thought they both liked it fine. It was flat-out dazzling.

"How about this one?" Frank pointed to a ring neither of them had picked, with a very small diamond you had to look hard to see.

The man put away the big diamond and pulled out the little diamond. He laid it on the pad without comment. Frank picked the ring up. "Sixty-nine dollars, huh?" he said.

"Yes, sir," said Bill. "Bit under a quarter of a carat." He drummed his fingers on the counter, then stopped.

"Well, what do you think?" Frank asked Arthur.

Arthur leaned in closer. "I like it a lot!"

"Sold!" Frank said to Bill.

The man nodded. "You picked yourself out a very nice ring."

Arthur could tell Frank was disappointed. He knew that, coming into the store, Frank had had big ideas that were cut down to size pretty quickly. It reminded Arthur of their dad, and he didn't ever want to think of his brother that way.

Frank took out a wad of bills and paid for the engagement ring. The jeweler put it in a little black-velvet box that made it look nice, and then they left the store.

"Are you all out of money now?" Arthur asked.

"Pretty near."

"I've got some saved. Not much. About eight bucks. It's yours."

"That's nice of you, Arthur, but no."

Arthur realized he wanted somehow to be involved with Frank and Mary, two people who were so much in love, who admitted freely their affection for each other. What would that be like, to be able to finally relax inside about loving someone? Thus far, his experience with love was that it felt like trying to run a hundred-yard dash while balancing an egg on a teaspoon.

They walked in silence for another block, and then Arthur said, "Mary has little hands, right? That ring you got will look beautiful on her. If you'd have gotten a big clunker, I think it would have looked tacky."

"I guess," Frank said.

He didn't sound convinced.

"She's going to be so surprised," Arthur said. "Are you going to get down on one knee?"

"In fact, I am."

"Can I come?"

"No!"

"When are you going to do it?"

"Soon," he said, and his jaw tightened, and he said nothing more. Arthur thought it had to do with that baby growing inside, getting bigger every day. Frank was in trouble, but also he was in love, and that would eventually take care of everything else. He wanted to talk to his brother about Nola, tell him what Mrs. Crawford had said about Corky Daniels. But this was his brother's time, and if Frank wanted to be quiet, why, that was just fine.

When they got home, their mother told them to wash up, dinner would be ready in fifteen minutes. Their dad was home, resting, so be quiet on the way upstairs.

After Arthur washed up, he found Frank sitting on the edge of his bed, staring at the ring. He looked up when he saw Arthur. "It's not so bad," he said.

Arthur came to sit beside him. "I like looking at it when it's not with all those other rings."

"Right, it looks a little better without the competition."

"I think it's beautiful," Arthur said.

Frank took the diamond ring out and put it on his pinky. "It does sparkle pretty good," he said, turning his hand this way and that.

"Boys?" their mother called from the foot of the stairs.

Frank quickly shoved the ring back into the box. He put it in his dresser drawer, under a pile of T-shirts.

"When are you going to tell Ma and Pop?" Arthur asked.

"After I ask Mary. Have to make sure she says yes."

"Ho," Arthur said. "Like she would say anything else."

Frank smiled.

They clattered downstairs, just like they always did, and it came to Arthur that even after Frank was gone and moved in with Mary, he would still clatter down these steps with Arthur. Even when Arthur too was gone from this house, there the brothers would be.

Chapter 19

THE NEXT SATURDAY was a rainy day, so Arthur wouldn't be working for Mrs. Crawford. He stayed in bed longer than usual, reading from one of his tree books. He liked the Westerns Frank had given him, but they didn't talk about baobabs living to be three thousand years old, growing seventy-five feet tall, and having trunks whose diameters measured sixteen feet. Reading that made him close his eyes for a minute, trying to imagine it. The natural world was better than anything. He couldn't say in words what it gave him, but he could feel it the minute he stepped outside: a kind of expansiveness and peace.

When he came down to breakfast, his mother told him that Mrs. Trentino had just called; she needed his help today.

"For how long?" Arthur asked.

"She didn't say. But you don't have any plans, anyway, do you?"

He and Harvey had talked about trying out hitch-hiking today. Just to the next town over, at least for the first time. Then they might go to St. Louis. But, "Not really," he said.

He could be stuck at that old lady's house all day. There was something about rainy days that could inspire women to come up with all kinds of projects for other people to do. Frank and Arthur had once spent a whole day cleaning the basement on a rainy day. And for what? Next week, the same old spiders and cobwebs, the bread-and-butter pickles mixed in again with fruit preserves and stewed to-matoes, the dank smell back in full force.

After he ate breakfast, Arthur called Harvey and told him their plans for Project X would have to be resched-uled. "That's okay," Harvey said. "It's raining, anyway. Nobody would want to pick us up because we'd get their car seats wet. I gotta go and visit my aunt and stay over-night. You should go to the movies when you're done working. Tell me what happens."

"I'll wait for you to go another time."

It grieved Arthur that he went to the movies with Har-vey and not with Nola, but this was still the state of af-fairs. Instead of holding hands with her, he endured Harvey's arm farts—Harvey thought it was funny to do that at the movies. He liked it when the patrons looked around while trying not to show that they were looking around.

At his mother's insistence, Arthur wore a raincoat and galoshes on the way to Mrs. Trentino's, and he hoped no one he knew would see him. There were huge puddles in the middle of the street and standing water on all the lawns. The rain had stopped just before he went out, but here it came again. Used to be he would love a rainy day like this. He and Frank would make paper boats and float them down the gutters.

It took Mrs. Trentino a long time to get to the door after Arthur knocked. She greeted him, then told him to put his wet things on some newspaper she'd laid out on the floor. She was wearing a faded apron over her blue housedress, and well-worn slippers. One of her earrings was hanging far down on her earlobe. He didn't want to embarrass her by calling it out, so he touched his own ear to send a hint. No go.

"Your earring is loose," he told her, and pointed.

"So what?" But she tightened it. "Come on, then," she said, and Arthur followed her into the kitchen. She gestured to a chair at the little wooden table, and he sat down.

She sat opposite him and for a long time said nothing. Arthur felt a small rising up of panic. Had she forgotten that she'd asked for him to come? But then she said, "How about some cookies?"

Ah. "Well, I just finished breakfast. Maybe later. But what can I do for you today?"

"What, are you in a rush?"

". . . No."

Yes.

"Let me tell you something, Arthur. Life can turn out a

way you never thought. Very, very different from what you thought."

"Yes, ma'am."

She rearranged herself in the chair, then asked, "Do you notice anything?"

He looked around the room.

"About *me*. Do you notice anything different about me?"

He studied her as politely as he could. "No, ma'am."

She pointed to her mouth.

"Oh," Arthur said. "Now I do." He had noticed right away that her mouth was a little caved-in-looking, but he hadn't wanted to embarrass her.

"It's my teeth."

"Uh-huh."

"I can't find them."

"Uh-oh."

" 'Uh-oh' is right. I have looked high and low, and they are nowhere to be found. And yet I know they're here somewhere. They didn't go walking out of here. So I thought maybe I'd hire some new eyes. Will you look for me, Arthur?"

"Sure." Finally: his mission for today.

"I already looked in the trash. And in my dresser draw-ers. On the bathroom floor, too; even under the tub." She looked over at him, and she was tearful now. "Just look for me, would you? They cost a lot of money."

"Of course, right away."

"If you don't find them, I'll still pay you."

"I'll find them."

He stood and cleared his throat. Where to begin? He lifted the curtains at the window. "Probably silly to look there, huh?"

Mrs. Trentino shook her head. "Absolutely not; already you're doing a good job, Arthur. I hadn't thought of looking there."

"Okay."

"You're a good boy, aren't you?"

"I don't know. I guess so."

He looked carefully under the table, ran his hand along the top of the refrigerator. He looked under the bananas in the fruit bowl. He looked on top of the stove, then *in* the stove.

"You never know, right?" Mrs. Trentino said. She was sitting at the table resting her chin in her hand now, watching him like he was a show on television.

"You say you looked in the trash, right?" Arthur asked.

"Yes. *All* the trash cans. You don't need to go digging in there."

"Then I guess I'll go and look in the other rooms."

"I'll come with you."

She stood slowly, and then they went into the living room, where Mrs. Trentino turned on the radio. "There. We'll have a concert."

She sat on the sofa and hiked her legs up onto the hassock stationed before it. "I got the edema," she said, poking at her ankles. "See?"

Arthur didn't see anything. Was edema good? Bad? "Uh-huh," he said, neutrally.

When he began moving around some framed photographs, she said, "See that guy there? In the big silver frame? That's my brother. He moved away; he lives in Florida. Once I visited him there. It was like paradise, I'm telling you: the big birds and the blue water and the poofy clouds. He said to me, 'Fina, why don't you move here?' I just laughed. But now I don't know why I laughed. I don't know why I *didn't* move there after my husband died. Bless his soul." She crossed herself and kissed her fingers.

"You could move there now, couldn't you?" Arthur carefully put the lid that he had dislodged back on the candy dish. Butterscotch was in there, his favorite.

"Move to Florida now? For what? My brother died a year ago and you don't want to know about his wife. Though I could tell you some things."

She pointed at Arthur, who was pulling open one of the top drawers in the china cabinet. "Ah-ah-ah! Don't go in there. They're not in there. I looked."

He moved on to the overstuffed chairs and lifted the cushions. Strange, he thought; he was kind of enjoying this. He found a quarter beneath one of the cushions and showed it to Mrs. Trentino.

"What is it?" she asked, squinting.

"Twenty-five cents."

"Huh. Mrs. Rockefeller. Put it in the ashtray."

"But anyway, I was saying about my brother. I told him *once* about how that woman he was ready to marry was bad for him. Once only. He was my brother; I had the right to share my opinion. But then what could I do? They were joined together in holy matrimony, and so . . ." She made the key-turning-the-lock sign at her lips.

"I guess he loved her. All his life, he loved her." She looked over at Arthur. "Who can account for why people love the ones they do? It's not a science."

"Nothing under here," Arthur said, after kneeling down to peer under the chair.

"Take a rest," Mrs. Trentino said. "Sit down."

He sat, though he didn't need a rest. He put his hands on his knees and tried to look cheerful.

"Do you have a girlfriend, Arthur?"

"Yes, ma'am."

"What's her name?"

"Nola." Now he'd done it. Mrs. Trentino probably knew her.

"Is she pretty?"

Nope, she did not know Nola. Everybody who knew Nola knew she was a knockout.

"Yes, she is very pretty."

"Is she a blonde?"

"No, her hair is black."

"Good. Too many blondes, and then if they're not blond, there they go with the bottles pouring poison all over their heads. Dark hair is better. It gives a mysterious presence."

Mrs. Trentino had been dark-haired; there were pictures of her from then. Now she was all white, and if you walked behind her you saw a flat, nearly bald spot near the top of her head.

Mrs. Trentino lifted her chin and frowned. She said,

"I'm going to tell you something now you won't believe. Nobody ever believes it. Your girlfriend won't stay pretty for long. I myself was a hot tomato, but look at me now.

" 'Pretty' goes away, but what can come in its place is 'beautiful.' And that's better. Do you know what I mean, Arthur? Because when you look with the eyes of love, what you see is beautiful. Even an ugly dog—you know what I mean. You've probably seen Mr. Blesoff and his terrible little dog that I don't even know what it is. But Mr. Blesoff acts like he's Lassie.

"What matters is not what girls look like, even though I know, I know: you're young, you like the pretty girls, you got the engine running. But what matters is who they *are*. In their soul. What you want, Arthur, is someone you see eye-to-eye with. Someone you can laugh with. But most important, you want someone you can cry with. All right, enough said. Let's get back to work. Where should we go next?"

"The bedroom?" Arthur asked.

Her eyes widened. "I haven't made my bed yet. Let me go in there and make my bed, and then you can come and look. Wait in the hall."

He waited in the hall. "Maybe you should look in the sheets," he called to her.

"What?"

He repeated it, louder.

"Good idea." A moment, and then, "Nope."

They looked around the rest of her house, and Arthur lifted every doily, looked behind and beneath every piece of furniture. In each room, Mrs. Trentino told him another story, like her house was a museum and Arthur had paid to come in. In the guest room: "See that bed? That is where my sister went into labor when she and her husband came to visit for Christmas. Her son was almost born *right there*. He was three weeks early. But we got her to the hospital just in time."

Finally, Arthur had looked everywhere. At Mrs. Trentino's suggestion, he searched the dining room one more time for good measure. He opened the doors to the china cabinet, and Mrs. Trentino pointed to the display of plates. "Aren't they beautiful? See the gold around the rim? Twenty-two karat. You wouldn't believe how many people I've fed off them. Most of those people are dead now. But the plates look brand-new, don't they?" She came over and gently closed the doors. "Okay. That's enough. We tried."

When she tried to pay Arthur, he refused.

"Never mind, you're a good boy," she said, holding out a couple of dollars.

"That's okay," Arthur said. "Maybe you could put that money toward the next job I do for you." She was kind of a crazy old lady, but he had enjoyed being with her today.

She peeled off one of the dollars and stuffed it in his shirt pocket. She said, "I enjoyed talking to you, Arthur."

"Thank you."

"Thank *you*."

She put her hand in her apron pocket and gasped. "Oh, my! Will you look at this?" She held up her dentures, wrapped in Kleenex.

"Huh," Arthur said. "*There's* your teeth!" They both smiled.

"See you," he told her, and closed the door quietly behind him. It occurred to Arthur that she might have hidden her dentures in her apron pocket, then used missing teeth as a ruse to have his company. If that were so, he was kind of flattered. But, also, if that were so, he was learning a lot about the kind of loneliness some people endured. He resolved to visit Mrs. Trentino soon, just to say hello. That's how he'd put it. He'd ring the bell, and when she answered he'd say, "I was just passing by, and I thought I'd see how you are." He imagined she'd put her hand to her breastbone and then let him in.

Outside, the skies had cleared and the earth was putting out that rusty smell that can come after a rain. Arthur decided he'd go to the Saturday matinee after all, and then head home.

He was settled in his seat watching the newsreel when he saw Nola come in with Ed Christianson, who was a senior. Ed put his arm around her right away.

Arthur didn't want to stay anymore. He felt a little bad about wasting the money, but he left. He didn't want to see those two heads together, in the dark.

He walked toward home quickly. The rain had cooled the day off, and his raincoat didn't offer much warmth. Here came another cold, he imagined. When he passed Mrs. Crawford's house, she was sitting out on her screened-in porch. "Arthur!" she called. "Come here for a minute, I want to show you some sketches of rosebush beds I'd like to add way out back."

He went gladly. Something to take his mind off things. *Things* being Nola.

He let himself onto the porch and took off his raincoat, then settled into a wicker chair beside her.

"How are you?" Mrs. Crawford asked. She looked so pretty, wearing a white dress with a navy cardigan over her shoulders, her hair held back with a scarf. He thought about what Mrs. Trentino had said, about pretty not lasting for long. But a guy couldn't help admiring it while it was there.

"Guess I'm kind of blue," Arthur said.

Mrs. Crawford lifted her pack of Lucky Strikes from the table, shook one out and lit it, and blew the smoke straight up toward the ceiling.

"I'm feeling a little blue, too," she said.

"Really?"

"Yup."

"How come?"

"Oh, you know. Rainy day . . ."

It occurred to Arthur that the news about her husband probably wasn't good. But he wasn't going to ask. Instead, he'd share his own grief. Sometimes listening to somebody else's woes could make your own weigh less.

"I just went to the movies and saw Nola there with another guy. He put his arm around her." One of his knees started jiggling and he made it stop. "My brother, Frank, he says I might need to make Nola jealous. He thinks I should tell her I might be interested in someone else. Do you think that's a good idea?"

"Hmm," Mrs. Crawford said. "Well, I wish I could tell you it's a *bad* idea, because I really believe in honesty.

That's the foundation for a really good relationship. But I would not be honest if I didn't say that sometimes it does seem to work, making someone jealous. It's a kind of game-playing a lot of people do. The question to ask yourself is, would *you* be comfortable doing that? And is it risky? In other words, if you say you're interested in someone else, would Nola abandon any feelings she might have for you?"

"I don't know if she *has* any feelings for me, though. That's the problem. She's *friendly* and all—she tells me things I don't think she tells anyone else—but . . ." He couldn't think how to explain his frustration. He saw it like this: He and Nola had been in a big field with lots of other people. He'd called her name and gotten her attention; she'd turned toward him and stood there. He'd waved for her to come over and she'd taken a few steps forward. A few. Then she'd stopped again, but her eyes were on him. What *did* a fellow have to do to move things forward?

He made his voice go cheerful. "So you have some new plans for the garden?"

"Yes. But before that, can we talk a bit more about Nola?"

He looked over at her, full of hope "Yes, ma'am."

"I'm sure it must have been hard for you to see her with another boy, but it doesn't mean anything, really. I think Nola sounds confused. She's just trying different things because she hasn't settled on what she really wants. She hasn't even *seen* what she really wants; sometimes it's hard to do that. Also, girls can sometimes run *from* what they want most to run *to;* I can't tell you why except to say that when that happens, it's a problem with them, not with you. I'll bet that in time she'll come around, Arthur. If nothing else, I think you'll become the best of friends."

That's not what he wanted. He wanted to be the guy standing in the dimness by their kids' beds as Nola kissed them, and then he would kiss them, too. "Night," he'd say. Why did that single word offer so much comfort? He guessed it was because it said so much. Home. Safety. The prospect of another day together as soon as morning came. He wanted to walk down the stairs to the living room afterward, and sit with Nola in the lamplight and talk. He guessed he was crazy. No wonder he was so comfortable with Mrs. Trentino.

He was comfortable with Mrs. Crawford, too. He realized now that both women had become his friends, same as Harvey. You didn't have to be a guy chucking a football to another guy to have a friend. You could have an odd boy and a crazy old lady and a beautiful young woman for friends. You could have your brother, the guy you could say anything to and ask any question of. You could even have the turned earth of a garden where you were planting all kinds of things you couldn't wait to see come up.

In the end, Arthur thought, it was up to him to decide what was what in his life. So long as he knew the truth about himself, for himself, maybe he would be okay.

Chapter 20

Arthur was at his locker in school on Friday afternoon when Becky Reed came up to him. She leaned against the locker next to his and smiled. "Hi, Arthur." Her voice was all curlicued.

"Oh!" Arthur said. "Hi."

She pooched her mouth a bit and lifted a shoulder, and he figured that Nola had talked to her: despite his reservations, he had decided to tell Nola he might be interested in Becky. Nola had looked quickly over at Arthur when he told her that and said, "Really? Becky Reed?"

"Yeah," Arthur said. "She's kind of cute."

"I guess so," Nola said. "Not very good at home ec, though."

"Oh, no?"

"No, I have to help her with sewing all the time. Last week, I had to help her so much I hardly got my own dress done. Oh, I did finish it, and I got an A on it."

"That's great, Nola."

"Becky has a little bit of a harder time." Nola's face had been set into a kind of soft pout and Arthur had thought, *It is working then?*

"Got any plans this weekend?" Becky asked.

She sure was making it easy for him. Well, Nola didn't have any problem dating other guys, and Frank had told him that he had to make Nola jealous. So he smiled back at Becky, who *was* a pretty cute girl: a spattering of freckles across her nose, curly blond hair. She had a space between her two front teeth that bothered Arthur, but when he had confided that to Harvey Guldorp, Harvey had shaken his head sadly like he was at a funeral and said, "Arthur. That is considered *sexy*."

"Really?" Arthur had asked, and Harvey had answered with a question of his own: "Good grief, Moses, what would you do without me?"

Now Arthur said to Becky, "Plans this weekend? I guess that depends on you." It came right out, something that someone far more confident than Arthur might say. Then, since he'd gone that far, he raised his arm to lean it up against the locker, right over Becky's head. He stood very close to her, like he'd seen other guys do, wishing he'd put on at least a little of his cologne that morning. *Look 'em right in the eye,* Frank was always telling him. Arthur looked down into Becky's face and held his gaze steady. He wanted to appear as nonchalant as a guy in a Zane Grey novel, but that wasn't how he felt. He felt like he was waiting in line to get a shot. He hoped he wouldn't start perspiring.

Becky was still smiling. "What do you mean it depends on me?"

"Well, how about going out with me tonight?"

"Really?"

What Arthur wanted to say was, "Well, no; sorry." But that would be awfully mean, and anyway, Frank's advice had always been good. Arthur would follow through with this and see what happened. He recalled the maze the fortune teller had told him he'd go through with Nola. He also recalled Frank quoting Shakespeare: *The course of true love never did run smooth* and *All is fair in love and war.*

So, "Yup, tonight," he said. "Sorry for the short notice."

"That's okay, I don't mind," Becky said. She tossed back her curls. "So! Where would you like to take me?"

Arthur had no idea. "Tell you what," he said. "Just give me your address and I'll come for you at seven o'clock."

"Okay. This is *exciting*!" She wrote down her address and phone number and pushed the scrap of paper into Arthur's shirt pocket, patting it twice. She started to walk away and then turned around. "I assume I'll be dressing up?"

Arthur thought of Nola, with her bare feet in the river, mindless of the mud she got on her skirt. He thought of the great pleasure he experienced just sitting outside with her, not going anywhere at all. "Sure, you can dress up," he told Becky.

He guessed he'd take Becky to the movies and then

somewhere else afterward, too. What with her getting dressed up and all. It was a good thing he hadn't given all his money to Frank. Women were expensive!

Arthur walked to class, thinking about how, if he had to spend money, he'd much rather spend it on Nola. But if Frank was right, he *was* spending it on Nola.

After school let out, Arthur pushed through the heavy front doors and saw Nola getting into a car with a bunch of other kids. She sat in the front seat, next to the guy driving. Arthur couldn't see him very well, so he didn't know who he was. But he was driving; he had a car, or could borrow one. And then Nola leaned over and kissed his cheek and the guy hadn't even given her anything. Or maybe he had. What did Arthur know?

He imagined sitting next to Becky Reed in the movies to try to make himself feel better. It didn't work. He needed to ask Frank if you could force yourself to care about someone. Because that's what he wanted to do, suddenly: just switch all his affection to someone who seemed to want it.

That night after dinner, Frank and Arthur went directly upstairs to their room. Arthur said he needed to get ready for his date, and Frank said he had to get started on a term paper.

Frank sat on the side of his bed and watched Arthur change clothes. "So you're taking another girl out, right?" Frank asked.

"Yup."

"Good for you. I've got big plans tonight, too."

"For writing your term paper?"

"Nope."

"For what, then?"

"For proposing to Mary. I've been thinking about this. She's told me that her favorite scene in literature is when Juliet comes out on the balcony and asks where Romeo is. You know that scene, right?"

"We haven't done that play yet."

"Well, in *Romeo and Juliet,* it's late at night, and Juliet comes out onto her balcony. She's missing Romeo—just longing like crazy for him—and then there he is. I'm going to call Mary to come outside and ask her to marry me. I think she'll love it."

"You're going to wake her up?"

"Yes."

"What if she's cranky because you woke her up?"

"She won't be."

"Won't she be in her pajamas? I thought you wanted it to be romantic."

"It will be romantic! Juliet's in her nightgown when Romeo shows up!" Frank was getting a little angry, so Arthur backed off. But it seemed to him that if a girl was concerned about getting dressed up for a first date, she might not want to be in her sleepwear when she got proposed to.

Frank said, "Let me ask you something, Arthur. If you came upon Nola in her pajamas, would you be bothered by it? Would it change your mind about how you feel about her?"

He thought about this. "No."

"And why is that?"

"Well, because it would still be . . . *her*. I don't care what she wears. She's just . . . She's got a way about her. I can't explain it."

"Don't have to. It's how Mary and I feel about each other. I know she's beautiful, but I don't even see her anymore. I see her soul. I *feel* her soul. I want to spend the rest of my life with Mary. I feel like she's the place where I can put down my stuff, do you know what I mean? I can relax with her. I can show her things I've never been able to show to anyone else."

He shook his head. "Just talking about this makes me want to go over there right now. But I'll wait until later. I like the idea of it being really dark. More romantic."

"Stars," Arthur said.

"Now you're catching on."

"I'll see you when I get back," Arthur said, patting down his hair.

"Good luck," Frank said. "Be brave."

Arthur had no idea why Frank had said that; it made him a little worried. He walked to Becky's house, passing by younger boys out playing in groups, unmindful of women and their ways, unconcerned about how much money they had. When he got to Becky's house, he felt like turning around. He walked up the front porch steps like he was going to meet a firing squad. He was introduced to her parents, then to her two younger sisters, big-eyed twins about ten years old who giggled behind their hands for no reason that Arthur could see. He was instructed to have Becky home by ten.

Then Becky and Arthur were walking down the block together. "So where are we going?" Becky asked. "What's my surprise destination?"

Arthur told her they were going to the movies to see *The Egg and I*, then out for hot-fudge sundaes after that.

"Oh," Becky said, and Arthur could see she was trying not to show her disappointment. Well, what had she expected, he wondered, that he would whisk her off to Gay Paree?

She recovered soon enough, and took Arthur's arm and started yakking. The whole way to the Palace Theater, she wouldn't stop going on and on about the movie's stars. Did Arthur know Claudette Colbert had been born in France? Did he know she had studied fashion design? Did he know her real name was Émilie? And Fred MacMurray's face had inspired Captain Marvel's; wouldn't it be *dreamy* to have a comic strip character modeled after you?

"Why?" Arthur asked about this last, when Becky was coming up for air and he could get a word in edgewise.

"Why what?"

"Why would it be dreamy to have a cartoon character modeled after you?" He guessed he just wanted to be contrary.

"Well, *Ar*thur!"

He waited.

"It just would! Everybody knows that! Jiminy!"

They were walking past the Kiersons' place. The house,

which had been completely destroyed in the tornado, had been substantially rebuilt in the last couple of weeks, and Arthur stopped for a minute to admire it. "This place got flattened in the tornado," he told Becky.

"Where?"

He looked at her. "*Where?*"

"Yeah, where did it get flattened?" She was getting a little huffy again.

"Well, 'flattened' means . . . you know. It fell down. Flat. On itself. So that there was nothing left."

"Anyways," Becky said. "We should get going. I don't want to miss the previews. Do you like the previews, Artie?"

Well, this was worse than the dentist.

"I guess," Arthur said.

They walked the rest of the way to the movie in silence. After the usher seated them, Becky positioned her hand close to Arthur's. He was supposed to take it and hold hands with her, he supposed, but he hadn't the heart to do it. After the movie was over and they'd gotten outside, Arthur said, "I don't feel so good."

Becky looked at him, her eyes narrowed, her hand on her hip. "I thought so. I thought you were sick—or *something*."

"How come?"

"For Pete's sake, you didn't even try to take my hand or put your arm around me or *any*thing. Forget it. I'll just walk myself home."

As soon as Becky was out of sight, Arthur began to

run. Home, his room, and his brother had never seemed so good.

He found Frank upstairs, lying on his bed with his eyes closed. He didn't answer when Arthur whispered his name.

Arthur sat quietly at his desk and pulled out a sheet of notebook paper. Maybe he'd send Becky an apology; he'd been a jerk, he knew it. But on the paper, he wrote nothing. He just sat there, seeing a split image of Becky and Nola.

When Frank woke up, it was past eleven, and Arthur had just gone to bed.

"Hey, Arthur?" Frank whispered. "You awake?"

"Yeah."

"How'd it go with Becky?"

Arthur told him.

"Holy smokes. You deserve hazard pay. Did *any*thing good happen with her?" Frank asked.

"No. And she called me Artie."

"Well, we won't be too hard on her for that. Girls like to do that: make up little nicknames for you. It's actually a sign of affection."

"Does Mary have a nickname for you?"

"She does."

"What is it?"

"Oh, Artie, I can't tell you *every*thing."

Arthur lay back down. "When are you leaving?"

"Soon. I worked really hard on what I'm going to say."

"What *are* you going to say?"

"Nope."

"Come on. One word."

"Okay: 'Mary.' "

Arthur sighed. "I tell you everything and you tell me nothing."

"All right, all right. I'll tell you something. I'm going to stand outside her house. And then I'll . . ." He stopped talking.

"What? You'll what?"

Frank got out of bed and stood by the window, looking out, his arms crossed. "I'll call her name, real softly, till she hears me. And when she comes out, I'll tell her about the first time I ever saw her, and how I knew right away that she was the one. I'll tell her why I knew. And then I'll tell her that it doesn't matter where we live, that she is my home. And . . ."

He turned around. "Listen, Arthur. I don't want to tell you anything else. It's private. It *should* be private. I *will* tell you that I'm going to finish with a poem I wrote for her."

"Really? You wrote a poem for her?"

"Yup. I memorized it so I can recite it to her. And I'm *not* telling it to you."

"I *know*. But what's the first thing you'll do when she says yes?"

"What do you think?"

"Kiss her, of course. Hey! Maybe you should bend her way backward, like that sailor and nurse on V-J Day!"

"That was some kiss."

"Right! Do that!"

"I don't think I'll do that."

"What will you do?"

He shook his head and smiled. Outside, they heard a sudden fluttering of wings.

"Owl?" Arthur asked.

They heard the muted call of a whip-poor-will.

Frank said, "That's my cue." He went to his dresser and pulled out the little black-velvet box.

"Here. Let me practice." He put the box in his pocket, knelt before Arthur, and then removed it, opening it smoothly with one hand. Arthur could see a little sparkle from the diamond.

"Will you marry me, Artie?" Frank said.

Arthur raised his voice to a high pitch and fluttered his eyelashes to answer him. "Over and over again."

Frank raised an eyebrow. "Not bad." He put his finger to his lips, tiptoed to the door, and was gone. He didn't make a sound going downstairs or when he went out the back door. Arthur vowed to stay awake until Frank returned.

Chapter 21

ARLY THE NEXT morning, Arthur awakened to the sound of the telephone ringing. At first he was afraid it was Becky Reed calling. He'd practically had nightmares about her. He thought, *Oh, no, she's calling to see if I'm really sick, and my mom will tell her I'm fine.* He looked over at Frank's bed, intending to tell him what he feared, but it was empty, unslept in. Arthur supposed it made sense that Frank might have spent the whole night with Mary. She would have said yes to his proposal, they would have joyfully celebrated, and then maybe they fell asleep together. His brother didn't fear their father anymore; if Frank wanted to stay out all night, why, he would. But the next sound Arthur heard was his mother saying, "No! No!" and then *"Eugene!"*

Arthur ran down the stairs behind his father. When they got to the telephone table in the hallway, there was Arthur's mother standing and sobbing with her hands over her face, the phone's receiver dangling on its cord.

"Go and get Frank," Arthur's father told him, grimly.

"It's *about* Frank," Arthur's mother said. She resumed sobbing, *howling,* really. "He . . . He . . ."

Arthur's father walked slowly over and took his wife into his arms. "Shh, shhh, what happened?" he asked, his voice low and angry-seeming.

"He . . ." Her breathing was jerky. "They found him by the tracks. Oh, Eugene. A *train* hit him."

"What? What are you talking about? When?" He turned to Arthur. "Go up and *get* him."

"He's not there, Pop." Arthur could hardly hear his father. Everything inside him had gone distant.

His father tore away and ran upstairs, and his mother stood staring at the space before her.

"Ma," Arthur said. "Ma. Is Frank dead?"

She looked at him, and he saw the answer in her eyes. He stood stock-still.

His father came running back downstairs. "Where is he?" he asked. *"Where is he?"*

"The morgue at the hospital," Arthur's mother said. She spoke as though she had left her body and some automatic device was delivering the news.

Arthur's father picked up the dangling phone receiver. "Who is this?"

He listened, his eyes wide. Then, "Okay. Don't . . . I'll be right there."

He hung up, and for a long time, he stayed still with his back to them. Then he turned around and said, "You two stay here."

"I'm coming," Arthur's mother said.

"Please. I don't think you should. Let me take care of this. I don't think you should see him."

"I'm coming!" Arthur's mother said. "Of course I am! I'm his *mother*!" Her voice was loud now.

"All right," his father said. "All right."

"Arthur?" his mother said. "Get dressed. Hurry."

Arthur was grateful for this, at least. That he hadn't needed to speak to say that he was coming, too.

Chapter 22

ARTHUR TOOK A week off from school. During that time, it seemed as if he got almost no rest at all. He would fall asleep from pure exhaustion, but then he would wake up and there was Frank's empty bed, and he would start in crying again. He tried not to make any sound because he didn't want his parents to feel they had to take care of him. They were like husks of human beings, drifting slowly around a house with silent and darkened rooms, the shades all pulled. People came by with all kinds of food for them and they ate it dutifully, tasting nothing. Arthur and his dad helped Arthur's mother clean up the kitchen afterward and then all of them sat silently in their respective places in the living room. Sometimes the radio played in the background, uselessly.

Arthur didn't want to be there. But he didn't know where to go. Harvey had called to say how sorry he was, but Arthur could barely speak to him. His parents didn't want him sitting alone up in what was Frank's and his bedroom, but Arthur didn't see what difference it made.

The first couple of days, he and his parents had sat at the kitchen table and gone over and over what had happened. Arthur told his parents that Frank had been on his way to propose to Miss Anker, that they had been having a love affair. He wasn't sure he should share the fact that Mary was pregnant, but finally, reluctantly, he did.

There was an awful silence after Arthur told them that. Then his father said, "What are you saying?"

Arthur didn't know what his father meant. What he was saying was what he'd just said. But this was shocking news, he realized, and so he tried to be patient repeating it. "Miss Anker and Frank, they were in love. And they had a love affair. And Miss Anker is going to have Frank's baby."

"When?" Arthur's mother asked.

"I think in about six months," Arthur said.

"How do you know this?" Arthur's father asked.

Arthur shrugged. "Frank told me."

His father nodded, and his hands, which were clasped on the table, tightened.

His mother grew tearful. "But why didn't he tell us?"

"He was going to," Arthur said.

"Who else knows about this?" Arthur's father asked. And Arthur answered truthfully, saying he didn't know. But he guessed if people didn't know, they'd find out now.

"Oh, boy," his father said. "Boy, oh boy. Just what we need, on top of everything else, to have Frank's reputation—"

"Stop," Arthur's mother said. "Stop it! Who cares about that?"

"*I* do," said his father. "He's my son and I care about his legacy."

"He's my son, too," Arthur's mother said. She stood up and pushed her chair in. Her voice was trembling. "And you know what I care about? That part of him is still here."

She left the room, and Arthur's father got up to fill his coffee cup. When he sat down at the table with Arthur again, he asked, "What do think, son? Are the kids at school going to give you a hard time?"

"I don't know," Arthur said. "I guess I don't care. I guess I feel like Frank and Miss Anker loved each other, that's all. They didn't *hurt* anyone."

His father nodded. Then he looked at Arthur for a long moment. "You're going to take some flak. That's how people are. They're just going to jump all over this: 'Ohhhhh, Frank Moses got a teacher *pregnant*.'"

"I don't care," Arthur said. "I don't."

"Miss Anker is in for it, too."

"I don't think she'll care, either. There are bigger things she's thinking about."

"All right, then," his father said. "All right." He went to the doorway of the kitchen and called, "Are you upstairs?"

"Yes," his mother answered back faintly.

"I'm coming up," his father said, then stood still, listening. There was no objection and he started to leave the room. But he turned around to say, "Listen, son. You tell me if anyone . . . if they hurt your feelings. If someone says something terrible to you. Okay? If they bother you in any way. *Any*one, no matter who it is. And I'll take care of it."

"Okay, Pop." Arthur would do no such thing. It didn't matter what anyone said. It only mattered that Frank was not there anymore. A terrible everlastingness, his absence. Another kind of coffin, a coffin for the living.

The police had assured them that Frank didn't suffer: his death was instant. And Arthur had had the strangest reaction when he heard that. He'd remembered Frank once sinking a three-pointer from center court during a basketball game, then seeking out Arthur in the stands, dusting off his hands and grinning. *Done.*

Arthur's father was disabused of the idea that the "low-lifes" had had anything to do with this: the nature of Frank's injuries, the fact that the ring was still in his pocket. He hadn't been robbed and then pushed onto the tracks. He had made a mistake, pure and simple. But hadn't he seen the train coming? Arthur's mother had asked. Hadn't he *heard* it? No doubt, said the older of the policemen, a soft-spoken man whose face was full of compassion. But these things happened, he said; people saw a train and thought they could beat it and didn't. Most of them didn't survive, but the ones who did all said the same thing: "I thought for sure I had time. I didn't realize." Arthur felt sure Frank would have thought he could make it across, and he hoped the only thoughts his brother had before he died were of Mary and the happiness that lay before them.

In the days that followed, word did get out about Frank and Mary. Arthur's mother heard two women at the grocery store talking about Frank getting a teacher pregnant, but they clammed up quickly when they saw her. His father said no one said anything directly to him, but they were different around him. Awkward.

"It will pass," Arthur's mother said.

Arthur didn't tell his parents that the news was out all over school as well. Harvey Guldorp called and told Arthur that kids were acting like it was the most sensational thing ever to happen in the history of the world. If ever anyone tried to talk to Harvey about it—"You're friends with Arthur. Did he know? Did you?"—he told them to lay off. "But you know who's been sticking up for both Frank and Miss Anker?" Harvey said. "Nola McCollum. She tells kids who talk about them that it's none of their business. She says that they were in love, and these things happen." Harvey said Nola had been absolutely fierce a couple of times in her defense of Frank and Miss Anker, and then the kids had talked about *her* for a while.

"By the time you come back to school, it will all have died down," Harvey told Arthur.

"Uh-huh," Arthur said, and he heard the listlessness in his own voice.

The whole town seemed to be in mourning over the loss of Frank. The day after the funeral, where the church had been filled to capacity, Arthur went for a walk. He had to get out of the house. Everyone he saw offered him a sorrowful smile or muted condolences. It was terrible. The only good thing that happened on that walk was that he saw Nola through the window of Modernette, a dress shop where all the girls liked to go, and she was standing with Suzie Templeton, the girl who'd been tricked about the slumber party. Nola was holding a dress up to Suzie and smiling at her, and Suzie was smiling back to beat the band. *Huh,* Arthur thought. But that was all he thought. It was too hard to think about Nola or anyone else. He took in the sight of the trees, of the blue blank slate of sky, and of birds flying in formation, and his spirit stirred a bit. But then he went home quickly, back to the work of mourning. It *was* work. It was hard and heavy and painful, and, for the time being, anyway, it never stopped. It was *on* you first thing in the morning and last thing at night. It invaded your dreams. It stole your appetite.

Arthur was angry that his parents seemed to be doing so well. Oh, you could see the pain in their eyes, and they were quieter than usual, but they just kept *on* so *well.* His mother: turning on the radio first thing in the morning; washing clothes and serving breakfast, lunch, and dinner; pin curling her hair at night. His father: off to work the day after the funeral, though his company altered his route so that he could come home every night for a while. So his father came home for dinner, and he read the evening paper until he was called to the table, and then they all sat and ate, and his parents chatted. Arthur mostly stayed silent. Dinner did not make sense to him.

Once Arthur had opened the basement door and seen his mother sitting on the steps bent over a jar of preserves, softly crying. Arthur figured she didn't want him to know, and so he closed the door to the basement quietly. Since then, he'd noticed times when his mother wasn't around and the basement door was shut, and he gave her her privacy. He'd seen tears in his father's eyes once, when they passed in the hallway, but his father was careful not to let that happen again.

He knew what his parents thought of what they called cheap displays of emotions. He knew they believed in people keeping their sorrows to themselves, as so many did during World War II. *Stiff upper lip!* Arthur imagined them thinking. He didn't want them to hurt more, but he wanted to *see* their hurt. Or maybe he *did* want them to hurt more. He supposed that was awful of him. Fine—he was awful.

People came to the house to offer sympathy. Arthur got called out of his room to see Mrs. Crawford, who had come with a ham-and-scalloped-potato casserole and a packet of seeds that she gave privately to Arthur. "Forget-me-nots," she told him, and his breath went bumpy when he thanked her. Even Mrs. Trentino had made an appearance, lumbering into the kitchen to present the family with lasagna and garlic bread and a ricotta pie and to tell Arthur's parents that he was a good boy. Other people came to share memories of Frank, ones that highlighted what a swell guy he was: so funny, so kind, so smart. It reminded Arthur of Gold Star families who said they were so grateful to the men who had served alongside their sons and who, after those men got home, came to visit them. It was said that the men shared things that under other circumstances would have been meaningless but now were precious beyond words. One more glimpse of someone the families would never see again.

But Arthur hated it when people shared things about Frank. For one thing, he already knew nearly all of the stories: The time Frank was working at the grocery store and chased a guy for three blocks because he'd made a mistake and shorted the fellow the change he was due back. The time when Frank was a little guy, maybe seven, and had gone around the neighborhood ringing doorbells asking for a penny for a song. His athletic prowess, his academic promise, his contagious cheerfulness. The way he always picked the weak guys first to be on his team in gym class. And there was a smattering of misdeeds: The time he and his buddies went for a joyride in one of the dads' cars and introduced it to the base of a tree. The time this same group, led by Frank, had put the principal's desk in the parking lot of the school.

Arthur's parents seemed grateful to hear these stories even if they, too, knew them, but Arthur didn't need his neighbors telling him how exceptional his brother was. He felt he didn't need his neighbors, period: a kind of hatred of people—made no less vehement by its unfamiliarity— had come over him, an inability or unwillingness to tolerate anyone. Seeing or talking to other people only made him feel worse. Even his mother. One night she came up and sat beside Arthur as he lay in bed, staring at the ceiling. For a long time, neither of them said anything. Then Arthur said, "Are you mad at Pop?"

"For what?"

"For how he beat up on Frank?"

She swallowed. She was still wearing her apron after having done the dishes, and Arthur fixed his gaze on the floating spatulas and rolling pins and measuring spoons; he couldn't look at his mother after he asked her this question. She had to be mad at his father. She *had* to be.

But she said, "No, I'm not mad at him. Not now, anyway; his heart is broken just like yours and mine. He might be suffering even more than we are."

A derisive sound escaped Arthur, and he turned onto his side, away from her.

"Don't you think your father regrets the way he treated Frank? Even when he was doing it, he did. Oh, I used to get so angry at him; I think you know that. I just didn't know what to *do*. But then, as you very well know, your father started behaving so much better. And so now . . ."

She laid her hand gently on Arthur's back. "Marriage is a funny thing. It only *really* makes sense to the ones who are in it together, and not even always then. But here's what I want you to know, Arthur. I love your father not only despite his faults, but maybe *because* of them. Not that I ever wanted him to hurt Frank or you or anyone else. Not that I admire or condone a lot of his behavior. But he *reveals* himself to me in being the imperfect person that he is. And I do the same. I believe that when we show each other our frailties, or admit to our mistakes, we are asking not only for forgiveness but for help in changing. To me, that's what makes a *real* marriage. You forgive each other. You do for each other. You try to help each other be better people."

Arthur had no words to respond. Was he supposed to feel bad for a guy who'd regularly whaled on his son? His father's getting "better" was not enough. There was a time when Arthur was ready to forgive his father. But not now. Not now he wasn't. He closed his eyes and told his mother he wanted to be alone. He hated everyone, including her. And he hated everything: his room, his bed, the shirt on his back, the breeze coming through the window. Most of all, he hated the sound of the train whistle, which still came every day, as though nothing at all had happened. If ever he could hear that without dying a little himself, it would be something.

"Arthur?" he heard his mother say, but he didn't respond. She got up off his bed and left the room. Arthur opened his eyes and looked over at his closed door. It occurred to him that being this way was not getting him anywhere he wanted to be. And yet here he stayed. Another person to add to the list of those he was angry at: himself.

Late one afternoon several days after Frank's death, Arthur went to Mary's house. He knocked on the door, she opened it, and he fell into her arms. She invited him in and sat him at her kitchen table and asked how he was doing. Arthur answered honestly: "Bad."

"Me, too," she said. A couple of tears spilled over, and she quickly wiped them away. "I resigned today," she said.

Arthur knew that she had; Harvey had called and told him the whole school was buzzing about *that* now. But Arthur didn't want to tell her he knew. He didn't want her to know he was yet another person talking about her behind her back.

Arthur reached into his pocket and pulled out the ring Frank had bought. The funeral home had given it to the family, and his mother just left it on the coffee table until finally Arthur brought it upstairs and put it in Frank's top dresser drawer. But he had brought it with him to Mary's house, and now he opened the little velvet box and showed her. She sat unmoving, until he pushed the ring over to her.

"Oh," she said softly, gazing into the box. "An engagement ring. How beautiful." Her face was full of such longing.

"Do you want to put it on?" Arthur asked.

She did, and they both admired the way the ring looked on her hand. Arthur hoped she'd keep it on, but she returned it to the box and closed the lid. She started to give it back to him, but Arthur said, "I think he would have wanted you to have it, even if you don't wear it. I know he would. And I . . . Well, I do know a little about how he was going to propose to you. Do you want me to tell you?"

She held back a sob and nodded.

"He wouldn't tell me everything, he said it was private."

She smiled, then looked down at her folded hands, waiting, and so Arthur told her all he could remember about what Frank was going to do. "He wrote a poem for you, too," Arthur said, finally. He'd almost forgotten that part. How could he have almost forgotten?

Now Mary looked up. "Did he?"

"Yes. He didn't share it with me, but he was going to recite it to you."

"Oh, I wish I could have heard it."

"I know he worked on it for a long time."

"He was a gifted writer, your brother. I honestly think he could have made a living at it. I'm sure of it."

Arthur sat up straighter in his chair. Best to get to it.

"Mary? I want you to know that Frank told me about the baby. And I guess this might sound strange, but I'd like to let you know I'll be glad to marry you, if you want. I'm sixteen, so . . . That way, you wouldn't have to give the baby up."

"Oh, Arthur. My goodness. What a beautiful thing for you to offer. I'm honored, truly I am. But I'm not going to give up our baby. I'm moving back to my parents' house. After the baby is born, I'll find another job teaching, and my mother will look after our son. Or daughter."

Arthur loved that she still said "our." But, "You're moving away?" he asked. He was devastated to think he'd never see Frank's child.

"It seems like the best thing to do," Mary said. "It's a few hours away. I'll send you a postcard with my address once I'm settled. Okay?"

"Sure," Arthur said. "Maybe I can come and visit you." He knew, saying it, how impossible that would be. But he had to say it.

They sat awhile longer, mostly in silence, and then Arthur went home. He took the shortcut, over the tracks, as he had on the way over. Maybe it was a bad idea, but he wanted to go that way; he thought he might feel Frank there. But he didn't, not going and not coming home, nor did he see any evidence of the accident, as he'd feared he might. There were the tracks, the same as always. There was Frank, gone forever in a way Arthur still couldn't quite realize. It was as though he half expected his brother to pop out from the bushes and say "Ha, gotcha!" and Arthur would punch him as hard as he could and say "Not funny. *Not funny!*"

When he got back home, he told his parents he'd given the ring to Mary, and they said Arthur had done the right thing. He told them she was moving away, and his father nodded and said, "It's probably for the best." Arthur thought his father could say "black as coal" and what Arthur would think was *white as snow*. His mother said she was going to the cellar for potatoes.

The day before he was to go back to school, Arthur was sitting on the side of his bed after lunch, staring over at Frank's bed. Still empty. Ever empty. He walked over and slowly lay down there. He tried to feel what it had been like to be his brother, but how could he ever do that? Frank was so powerfully himself. No one would ever take his place.

When he heard a knock on the door, he sat up quickly and moved to his desk. Then, "Come in," he said.

His mother cracked the door open. "There's a phone call for you."

"Who is it?"

"It's Nola."

Arthur stared at her.

"I think you should take it," his mother said. "But if you don't want to, I could tell her you're sleeping."

"I'll take it," he said. "Just tell her I'll be right there."

His mother nodded and closed his door, and Arthur moved to the window and rested his arms on the sill. He looked out for a moment, hoping, he guessed, that something would come to him, but nothing did. He was still mostly vacant, dull-eyed, tamped down by a despair that would not go away. It was as though he were seeing everything through mesh.

But down the stairs he went, and when his mother saw him, she said, "I'll be out hanging laundry."

At the telephone table, Arthur sat on the little seat and said a low "Hello?"

"Arthur? It's Nola."

"Hi."

"Hi."

An awful silence.

Then both of them spoke at once, Arthur saying "How are you?" and Nola saying something else.

"Pardon?" Arthur said.

"I said, 'I've been wanting to call you, but I was scared. I didn't want to bother you.'"

Oh, he very nearly saw her standing there, pressing the receiver to her ear. Her black hair, her long lashes.

"I don't guess you could ever bother me, Nola," he said.

"So what have you been up to?" she asked brightly, and followed this immediately with "Oh, that was so stupid. What a stupid thing to say. I'm sorry."

"It wasn't stupid," Arthur said. "It's a natural thing to say. I haven't been doing too much, though."

"No . . ." Nola said.

"How about you?" Arthur asked.

"Just . . . you know. The usual. School, and . . . Oh! I'm on the decorating committee for the prom, so we've been busy trying to come up with a theme. I think it's going to be Enchanted Island."

"Enchanted Island, that sounds pretty interesting."

"Yes, lots of fanciful trees and flowers. Too bad you're not on the committee; I'll bet you'd have lots of ideas."

He'd have no ideas, actually. Not now.

He cleared his throat. Something was rising up in him, a creeping sorrow, a vague irritation, and he remembered now that this always happened whenever he let thoughts of Frank drift too far away. Reentry was jarring. You could get caught up in something but then you'd remember, and it was like walking into a wall. Easier to stay with grief than to try to forget it.

"I sure am glad you called, Nola." His tone was businesslike now.

"I'm glad, too, Arthur. I'm glad just to hear your voice. I've missed you. I went to the park the other day and I was looking at all the trees and thinking about when you told me about the redbud tree, remember that?"

A million years ago. "Sure, I remember."

"I'd never really looked—"

"Nola?"

"Yes?"

"I'm awful sorry, but I have to go, my mother's calling me to help her with something."

"Oh! Okay, well . . . I guess I'll see you when you come back to school."

"Thanks for calling."

"Arthur? I just wish I could help somehow. That's what I really wanted to say."

He hiked up his voice to offer an enthusiasm he didn't feel. "You did! I was really happy to talk to you."

"Okay," she said, but her tone was doubtful.

After they hung up, Arthur slowly climbed the stairs back up to his room. *Too hard,* he thought.

Eventually, life resumed. Arthur's father went back to his regular schedule for work and was gone four days a week. His mother went back to talking in friendly tones to anyone who called on the phone. She even went back to smiling, to laughing.

Not Arthur. He didn't smile anymore. And laughing? At what? He went to school, and then he came home and did his homework. Kids avoided him like kids always did when there was a death in a family. They didn't know what to say, so they said nothing. When he came down the hall, there was a ripple effect of eyes turning away. The only ones who tried to talk to him were Harvey Guldorp and Nola. Harvey asked again and again if Arthur would like to come over, or do something with him, and Arthur always said no. Nola came up to him on his first day back and said, "Oh, Arthur, I'm so happy to see you! It's wonderful to have to you back." Arthur nodded, but any words he might have said couldn't get past the tightness in his throat. He did manage "See you" before he turned to walk off to class. "See you!" Nola called after him.

The school year was almost over, and Arthur was glad. He supposed he'd get a summer job, and he hoped it would take his mind off things. Mostly, he woke up empty and went to bed the same way. After a while, it just seemed normal to feel that way. One afternoon, when Arthur was sitting out on the front porch steps, the tomcat that lived next door came over and sat beside him. He was a mess of a cat, half an ear missing, tufts of fur. He sat by Arthur and stared straight ahead. He didn't rub his head against Arthur or make one sound. He just sat there, staring. Him, Arthur could be with.

Chapter 23

IT HAD BEEN nearly a month since Arthur had looked over and seen Frank lying in bed with his hands clasped behind his head. So long since his brother's desk drawer had been opened, the books on his shelf read. So long without Arthur hearing the sound of Frank's voice. He was so afraid he'd forget it.

Today he'd be going to Mrs. Crawford's, where he was working half days for the summer. She went easy on him, not talking to him except to discuss the work she wanted done, letting him come and go when he pleased. He knew she was leaving it up to him to talk about what had happened, or not.

One morning, he'd been late coming downstairs for breakfast. His mother had left a note resting against the salt and pepper shakers: *Good morning, sleepyhead. I've gone to the grocery store.* She had left out a box of shred-ded wheat, a bowl, and a spoon, but Arthur didn't want to eat. He went outside and sat on the back steps, his hands hanging between his knees. He looked around at the yard, the trees, and felt the same odd sensation he'd been feeling since Frank died. Beneath him were the same back steps that had always been there, but they didn't *feel* like his back steps. And this house didn't feel like his house, this yard didn't feel like his yard. His body was irrelevant— silly, even. Everything was foreign and wrong. His head stayed fixed in one place; his eyes were open and looking at things, but he was seeing nothing. Who was the one he could talk to about all this? The one who was forever gone.

He walked to Mrs. Crawford's, and found her inspecting a rosebush when he arrived. She looked up at him, shading her eyes from the sun. "Good morning, Arthur!"

He managed a reply, then asked, "Is something wrong?"

She nodded. "Looks like rose rust. We'll have to get after that before it spreads."

"Okay."

He walked over to the bush and saw the characteristic yellow patches on the leaves. He would need to cut out the affected areas and burn them in the big black metal barrel Mrs. Crawford kept for that purpose.

He finished in less than an hour and went to knock at Mrs. Crawford's front-porch door. "All done," he told her when she came out. "I didn't see any more when I was out there. I guess we got it early."

"Good. That's a relief. It's always something with roses!"

"Anything else for today?" Arthur asked. He hoped there wasn't. Even Mrs. Crawford couldn't lift his heaviness.

"No, I'm pretty much caught up, thanks to you!" She opened the door. "Will you come and sit with me on the porch for a minute?"

"No, thanks," he said.

"It's not for lemonade, although you can have some if you want it."

He stood there.

"Please come in, Arthur," she said, and there was more authority in her voice now, and he walked through the door. She gestured to one of the wicker chairs and he sat down, staring at his knees.

"I wanted to talk to you about something," she said.

Great, he thought. *Another pep talk, another attempt to bring me around.* But what Mrs. Crawford said was "I lied to you."

Arthur looked quickly over at her.

"Remember when I told you my first love married someone else?"

Arthur nodded.

"That wasn't true. The fact is, he died of tuberculosis."

"Oh!" Arthur said. "I'm sorry."

"Thank you. I miss him still. That rainy day, when you and I sat out here, I had been thinking about him since I'd awakened. It still comes upon me, sometimes, the memory of all we might have . . ." She sighed. "Oh, he was wonderful. He was everything I wanted. I'd never met anyone

I was so immediately comfortable with. To say nothing of besotted by." She laughed. "I *was* besotted."

A silence fell between them, and then Mrs. Crawford said, "See, that's one of the reasons I garden the way I do. Because it helps me to understand better Eddie's dying." She sat with her head tilted, and Arthur imagined she was seeing Eddie's image. "When I'm out there, I'm face-to-face with what nature is, and that includes human nature, of course: cycles, beginnings and endings, death and then birth. Life goes on. Do you understand what I mean, Arthur?"

He said nothing.

"I think I might know what you're thinking, which is that you don't *want* it to go on; you want certain things in your life to be there forever. But, of course, it doesn't happen that way. Working in the garden shows me the naturalness of it all, helps me to see that as much as I might resist the notion, I'm only one part of a bigger picture. There is comfort in that for me.

"But here's something else, Arthur. As you know, my husband is ill. We're not sure what the treatment he got will do for him, but we were talking last night, and he said something I found extraordinary. I'd like to share it with you. Would that be okay?"

Arthur nodded.

"We were sitting out here, right where you and I are, and he all of a sudden said, 'You know, people think it's a sad thing to die, and I guess for some, or even most, it is. But I feel I've lived a very good life. And I don't mind making room for the next ones.' He took my hand then and I looked at his face and . . . Well, I guess this will sound silly, but he looked like an angel to me. Radiant. It was as though he'd been privileged to have some divine insight." She looked over at Arthur and smiled. "I guess that sounds crazy."

"No it doesn't," Arthur said. "Not at all."

"I believe he's come to peace about his own mortality. And that makes it a little easier for me, too. Not that I won't miss him, if this treatment fails, as it might. He's awfully weak right now. But him saying what he did opened up a discussion between us about how life is unsure, and risky, and how, although we seem to insist on counting on things—and depending on them, making all these assumptions that are not ours to make, really—the truth is that all anyone can do is take each day as it comes. To see life as an imperfect offering and focus always on making the best of what we have at any given moment. And to have faith in . . . well, whatever we can have faith *in*."

"Where is your husband?" Arthur asked, worried that Mr. Crawford might have overheard them from where he lay in bed.

But Mrs. Crawford said, "He's at work. Isn't he something? I guess that's what I wanted to say to you, Arthur. Despite everything, try to go back to work."

Arthur began to cry then, and she cried with him. After a while, Mrs. Crawford got them some Kleenex and they both wiped their eyes and Arthur told her he'd see her next Saturday.

He walked home slowly, and with each step he could feel life coming back to him. It wasn't a rush of happiness and good feelings; it wasn't close to the joy and ease with which he had once moved in the world. It was pain, was what it was, but he was grateful to feel it, because it meant an attachment to the world was beginning again. For better or for worse.

Arthur saw a familiar figure coming down the street: Harvey Guldorp. When they got close to each other, Arthur said, "Hey, Guldorp. How you doing?"

Harvey regarded him warily. "Okay. How about you?"

Arthur shoved his hands into his pockets, smiled, and nodded.

Harvey's face brightened. "Want to come over?" he asked. "I got a lot to tell you. A *lot*. My mom's not home. We can smoke."

"How's tomorrow afternoon?" Arthur asked. "Maybe one o'clock?"

"Sure." Harvey started to walk away and Arthur called him back and cuffed him lightly on the back of his head. "That's for nothing," he said.

Harvey punched Arthur on the arm. "Ditto."

When Arthur got home, he didn't feel quite ready to go into the house. His mother was in the kitchen on the phone, and he waved at her, then sat on the back steps and breathed out a long sigh. Behind him, the door opened, and his mother came out. She sat beside Arthur. "I got you some cherries," she said. "And I have a nice surprise. You know who just called for you?"

"No."

"I think you'll be pleased to know that it was Nola McCollum."

He held perfectly still, then managed, "Oh?"

"She asked if she could come and see you. I told her I thought it would be all right. But if you don't want to see her, I can let her know that. Otherwise, she'll be here in about fifteen minutes. Okay?"

He closed his eyes and said, "Yup."

His mother put her arm around his shoulders and gave him a squeeze. "Good!" she said, in her most normal, cheerful voice.

What would he talk to Nola about? The old conundrum. But she was coming, and he was glad.

Arthur went into the stable to feed Grimy, and when he came back into the yard, Nola was walking through the gate. Arthur's heart leaped up in that old way. She waved at him, and he waved back and walked toward her. She had a little smile on her face, but she also looked kind of scared. Arthur tried to look relaxed and friendly so she wouldn't feel that way. Gosh, she looked pretty, Nola Corrine, all in her light-blue summer dress, a blue ribbon tied in her hair. Cheeks rosy from the heat. He had forgotten how pretty she was.

When she stood before him, she said, "Hi, Arthur," and there was such warmth and caring in her voice that it made Arthur's throat hurt.

"Can we sit for a while?" she asked.

Arthur nodded, and she followed him to a corner of the yard that was relatively private.

They sat down in the grass, and Nola was very close to

him. For a while, neither of them said anything. Then Arthur said, "It must be killing you to have your shoes on."

She laughed. "Just about."

From the barn, they heard Grimy nicker and Nola said, "Is that your horse?"

"Yeah. Grimy."

"Is he? From the mud?"

"No, it's his name. Grimy."

Talking was like unsticking something. But it wasn't as hard as he thought it would be.

"What have you been up to?" he asked. And Nola leaned over and kissed him. It was so gentle, like a butterfly had brushed up against his mouth. Then she looked down and folded her hands in her lap.

"I've missed you a lot," she said.

"I've missed you, too." His voice caught, and he gave himself a moment. "It's just I've been . . ."

"I know. I wanted so much to invite you to come over or something, but I wasn't sure . . ."

"Yeah."

"And in school, seemed like you didn't really want anybody to talk to you."

"No. I guess I didn't."

"I wrote you a letter, but I didn't send it. I'm not a very good writer."

Frank, Arthur thought.

"And then I figured, *Well, I'll wait awhile and then I'll call and go over to see him.* So! You know. Here I am." She laughed a little.

"I haven't wanted to see anybody, but now that you're

here, why, it's . . . I'm very glad to see you. Thank you for coming."

"You're welcome, Arthur. What are you doing for the rest of the day?"

"Nothing. This morning I worked for Mrs. Crawford, in her rose garden. I don't know if you've ever seen those roses she has, but—"

"Oh, I have! She's famous for her garden; she's even been in the paper for it. I love her garden, and her house, too. When I was a little girl, I used to tell everyone that I would live there someday."

"Really?"

"Yup."

"It's a nice house, all right."

Arthur said that instead of what he was thinking, which was, *I have thought the same thing, that someday I'll live there. With you.*

"Arthur? I made you something."

She handed him a small package she had lying beside her, wrapped up nicely in green paper and matching ribbon. He hadn't noticed it until now.

"You want me to open it?"

"If you want to."

He started to tear the paper, then told her, "Thanks a lot, Nola."

"Wait and see if you like it," she said. "You might not like it. And if you don't, that's okay, I'll just . . ." She was leaning over to look at what Arthur was uncovering, almost like she was the one getting the present.

He finished taking the paper off and found a small framed watercolor of a tree. It was a redbud tree in bloom, a wild exuberance of pink blossoms, and between the branches of the tree was the blue, blue sky.

Arthur couldn't think of a single thing to say. It meant too much. It practically hurt his eyes to look at it. "Thank you," he said. "Boy, this is swell. I really like it, Nola."

"I'm not the best painter," Nola said. "But it's to tell you that . . . Well, I never do look at those trees now in the same way. Because of you."

Arthur lay the picture on his lap and studied it a bit more. Every blossom, painted by her. "Why, it's as good as the real thing," he told her. "It's better."

"No it isn't."

"It is."

Now she smiled fully. "I'm so glad you like it."

She looked at her watch. "I'd better go. I've got a baby-sitting job. Mrs. Tischler. She has five kids and they're wild animals. If I can keep them from burning the house down, I'll have done a good job." She stood. "So . . . bye, Arthur."

"Goodbye, Nola. Thanks for coming. And thanks for the painting!"

He got up and watched her walk halfway across the yard, and then she turned around. "Arthur? Would you like to come over and spend some time this evening? With me?"

He stood there.

"Never mind," she said quickly.

"No, it's just that . . . I mean to say that—"

"Well, I'm going to be home tonight," she said briskly. "So let's just say if you want to come by, we could go for a walk or something. I won't be mad if you don't come, Arthur. But I'll be happy if you do."

She closed the gate, waved, and started down the sidewalk.

Arthur went into the barn, where his dad kept his tool bench. He got a hammer and a nail and went up to his bedroom. On the wall above Frank's bookcase, he hung Nola's painting. Then he sat on the edge of his bed and stared at it for a while. "Look at that," he said out loud. "Look what Nola Corrine the Beauty Queen made for me." He was telling Frank, of course. Sometimes when Arthur told him things out loud, he could swear Frank was listening. This was one of those times. Arthur saw Frank listening with his head bent down a little, his arms crossed, his eyes crinkled the way they used to when he smiled. "Now you're getting somewhere," he would have told Arthur.

Arthur heard a knock at the door, and his mother poked her head in.

"Okay if I come in?" she asked.

"Sure."

His mother sat beside him. "Did you have a nice visit with Nola?"

He shrugged.

"You know, Arthur," his mother said, "in time, you will find that little bits of happiness will make their way inside you and stay there. One little thing, and then one thing more. And then you'll realize that you're okay. You'll be okay, son, I promise you. You'll never forget him and you'll never stop missing him. But you'll be okay. And for you to be okay doesn't take a single thing away from Frank."

Arthur hadn't realized he'd been thinking that way: that if he were happy, it would be disloyal to Frank. But now that his mother had suggested it, he saw that it was true.

His mother looked around the room and then smiled at him, the saddest smile. "I loved him so much. I was so proud of him. He will never be gone from me. I wish he lived somewhere besides in my heart, but I'm glad every day that he's still there. And, oh, Arthur, he wished for so much for you. I think the way for you to do right by him is to find a life of joy. Otherwise, I'll lose two sons."

She turned to face him fully. "You know, if I've learned anything in my life, it's this: you can push away everything but love. It will not leave. It will wait. Unto death, it will wait. You might as well accept it. You might as well give it freely, too—even more than freely. Anything else is pure exhaustion." She patted his knee and left, closing the door softly behind her.

Arthur lay down on Frank's bed. He clasped his hands behind his head and stared up at the ceiling, just as his brother used to. Something occurred to him. When a baby was born, they didn't have much choice in the matter: down the chute and here they were. But when you were already born, you could decide you were ready for life all over again, and then you got born in a different way. Just certain things had to happen, was all.

He looked up at Nola's painting and saw that it was very slightly askew. He leaped out of bed to right it. Golly. Nola McCollum had given him something right from her heart. Frank: *If they come around slow, they come around true.*

Chapter 24

ARTHUR GOT A little dressed up to go and see Nola. A plaid shirt, blue jeans, a nice brown belt. He wet-combed his hair into something resembling a decent look. He considered aftershave, but then remembered Frank telling him about it being too much. He'd go with the plain masculine scent.

When he left the house, neither of his parents looked up. He'd told them at dinner where he'd be going, and he guessed they wanted to give him some privacy.

Outside, everything looked bigger. And clearer. He hadn't been looking at much of anything the last several weeks, and now all that he saw seemed like it was stepping up to reintroduce itself: the Helmsleys' new Studebaker, the peonies in people's gardens so fragrant he could smell them from the sidewalk, a couple of young boys wearing pillowcase capes tearing around a front yard. He waved at people sitting on their porches.

Two blocks from Nola's, he saw Harvey Guldorp hopping down the sidewalk on a pogo stick. He was looking at his feet, concentrating, but when he heard Arthur calling his name, he looked up and hopped off his stick.

"Arthur!"

"Hi, Harvey. Where'd you get that?" Arthur asked, pointing to the pogo stick, admiring the metal pole with handles and footrests and a big metal spring.

"My aunt sent it to me," Harvey said. "She doesn't have any kids, so I get a lot from her."

"Is it fun?" Arthur asked.

"Crazy fun," Harvey said. He held out the stick to Arthur. "You want to try it?"

Arthur did, but he was shy to try it right out here on the sidewalk.

"If you fall, you won't fall far," Harvey said. "Give it a whirl."

Arthur stood on the pogo stick and immediately tipped over. "That's okay," he said. "I'll try another time."

"Suit yourself," Harvey said, "but it's pretty swell. Tell you what, we can go over to the schoolyard and you can learn there."

"I'm on my way somewhere," Arthur said.

"Where?"

"Going to see Nola."

"You are?"

"Yup. She invited me."

"She did?"

"Yup."

Harvey nodded gravely. "Well, I'm not telling you what

to do, Moses, but if you want I'll lend you my stick and you can show up there with it. Chances are, she'll be pretty impressed. And she'll be begging you to let her try it. *Everybody* wants to try these things."

"Another time," Arthur said.

"*Any* time," Harvey said. "I mean now that you're out and about and all. I can teach you to use this thing. I have to tell you, I got pretty darned good in just a week. I'm aiming for the world record."

"For *what*?"

"Number of jumps! Or maybe distance. After you get comfortable with it, you can actually go places with it. It's a little like having a car."

"I don't think you can break world records with a pogo stick," Arthur said.

"Oh, it'll happen. You'll see. Anyway, I'll see you tomorrow." He got back up on the pogo stick and hopped away.

A lot of kids at school dismissed Harvey Guldorp. Arthur had been one of them. But he was a pretty interesting kid, and good to have for a friend.

Arthur watched Harvey go down the street until he disappeared around the corner. Then he quickened his step to get to Nola's house.

When he arrived, the light was just beginning to fade from the sky, and a long smear of cloud was colored a soft pink. He stopped to look at it, watching until the color began to give way to the blue-purple dusk. Then he climbed the steps to Nola's door and rang the bell.

For a long time he didn't hear any sound, but then the

door opened, and there she was, Nola Corrine the Beauty Queen, in pin curls, blue jeans, and a plaid blouse. Except for the pin curls, they could practically be twins. "Arthur!" she said, and she seemed so surprised he wondered if he'd misheard her about coming over tonight.

"You did invite me over, right?" he said.

"I did," she said. "But I was so sure you weren't going to come! Didn't seem like you really wanted to."

They both spoke at the same time then, Arthur saying, "I *did* want to," and Nola saying, "But I'm glad you're here."

She put her hand up to her head. "Gosh. Look at me. I'll go upstairs and take out these bobby pins."

"You don't have to do that."

"Well, it's awful rude."

"It's not rude! You're just curling your hair. I don't mind. I get to see what you'd look like with short hair."

She smiled and struck a pose. "Well?"

"You look real nice."

"So . . . would you like to sit out here?" She was gesturing to the porch swing. Arthur had had a number of fantasies about Nola, and one involved just that: them sitting on her porch swing together, canoodling. In that fantasy, she was not wearing pin curls; her black hair was falling over her shoulders, and she was leaning over for a kiss, her hands on Arthur's shoulders. It wasn't a quick, friendly peck like she'd given him in his backyard. No, this was a real kiss, a long one. It embarrassed him to be recalling that now. He hoped she couldn't read his mind.

Arthur sat at one end of the swing, in case she didn't want to get close. Nola sat in the middle—not too close, not too far away.

"So," Arthur said, and immediately drew a blank. Maybe he should have taken Harvey up on his offer to borrow the pogo stick.

Nola smiled at him encouragingly.

Was this his moment to kiss her? She didn't move any closer, so he said, "Harvey Guldorp got a pogo stick."

"Who?"

"Harvey Guldorp? He's in our class at school."

"Oh, yeah, I think I know who he is. Black glasses? Kind of short?"

"That's him. I just ran into him, and he was out on his pogo stick."

"A pogo stick! I'll bet they're fun. I wish I could try one!"

You had to hand it to Harvey. Sometimes he knew what he was talking about.

"I'm sure I can arrange it," Arthur said, all smooth like he was the man in the Brylcreem ad. "How's your summer been?" he asked.

She sighed. "Not great. I've been babysitting a *lot*, trying to earn some money to buy new clothes for next year. I can't believe we'll be juniors. Almost seniors!"

"I kind of hated for this year to be over," Arthur said quietly.

He said it because last year was associated with Frank, and next year wouldn't be. He doubted Nola would understand that, but she said gently, "Because of Frank. Right?"

There it was again. The hurt.

"Hey, Nola. Want to go for a walk?"

She pointed to her pin curls.

"Can't you wear a scarf over them?" He'd seen women do that lots of times.

She hesitated, but then she said, "Okay, why not?" and went into the house. She came out wearing a flowered scarf she'd knotted at the back of her neck. It made her look even prettier, and he told her so.

She laughed. "Only you, Arthur."

"I'm not kidding. You look like that movie star who wears her hair over one eye."

"You mean Veronica Lake?" Arthur could tell she was pleased.

They set off together. Arthur thought it felt good just to walk by her side, and to look around her neighborhood, which was nicer than his: bigger houses, fancier cars in the driveways.

After a while, Nola said, "Arthur? Are we going anywhere?"

At first Arthur got a little excited, thinking she meant was their relationship going anywhere, which Frank told him girls liked to ask about all the time. "You gotta be careful with that one," he'd said. "You don't want to be rude, but you don't want to offer false hope." But then Arthur realized she meant out on their walk, were they going anywhere.

"I hadn't thought of any place in particular," he said. "I like to just roam around sometimes. See what happens."

"Me, too!" she said.

Someone came around the corner then, Steve Linsky. He was a year ahead of them, the studious kind, horn-rimmed glasses and a show-off vocabulary. But he was a good-looking guy, and Nola's gaze fastened onto him in a way that Arthur found discouraging. When they met up in the middle of the block, he spoke to Arthur first.

"Hi, Arthur, how are you? I'm awfully sorry about your brother."

"Thanks."

"What are you doing?" This he asked Nola.

"We're just out walking," she said. "It's a nice night for a walk, don't you think?" Arthur thought, *Please don't ask him to come along.*

"I've got pin curls in my hair," she told Steve, laughing a little and pointing at her head.

Steve didn't laugh. "Yeah, I noticed," he said. Nola flushed, and Arthur felt bad for her.

"Good to see you, Steve," he said, and took Nola's arm.

When they were too far away for Steve to hear, Nola said, "I think he was coming over to see me."

Arthur stopped walking. "Oh. So . . . you want to go back?"

"No. He's done that before, just shown up at my house. I think it's rude. And, anyway, I want to be with someone who doesn't make me feel terrible about my hair being in pin curls."

"I'm your man," Arthur said, and the words gave him the inside shivers.

"You're so relaxing to be with," Nola said.

"I'm glad."

"You might be the best friend I ever had."

Best friend.

"Nola, I care an awful lot about you," Arthur said. He hoped that might get her thinking about him another way.

But she was lost in thought; he wasn't sure she'd even heard him. She said, "It's funny, Steve Linsky isn't the kind of guy I usually go for."

Arthur said nothing. Because he thought that what she was saying was that she *did* go for him.

They walked a fair distance, Nola talking about how Corky Daniels had turned out to be a real cad, and thank goodness Arthur had warned her about him, and what was the matter with boys that they would dishonor girls they said they cared about? They moved on to what subjects they were going to take the next year, and by then they had circled back to Nola's house. Just before she went in, as she and Arthur were standing at her front door, he reached over and touched her cheek gently. He looked into her eyes and sighed. "Nola, I wish you could know . . ."

He couldn't say it: *how much I love you.*

She held his gaze for a long moment, her expression both serious and searching. Arthur's chest hurt; he could hardly breathe.

"See you," he said thickly, and went down the steps and into the night, where the moon was full and the stars were coming out one by one, as though gathering to see what all was going on.

A little way down the sidewalk, Arthur turned around. He'd had a feeling that she'd still be standing there, and he was right. "Good night," he called.

Uncharacteristically, she said nothing, just stood there at the door, then slipped inside.

He wasn't quite ready to go home. It had felt good to be out and about, and he wanted to walk some more before it got too late. He was headed in the direction of the cemetery, and he decided to go there. Since they'd buried Frank, Arthur hadn't been to visit him. He hadn't felt he could. Now he thought he might be ready.

When he arrived, he had a little trouble finding the headstone. There was certainly enough moonlight to see by, but to Arthur's shame, he couldn't remember exactly where Frank's grave was. Finally, he recalled that it had been close to the big willow tree, and he headed in that direction. He found Frank's grave soon enough then, and it was the oddest thing, to see it again. Arthur thought of a hammer pounding in a nail: how the first taps are tentative, and then you drive it home. Standing there brought a kind of finality he had been avoiding. But it also brought comfort, because here his brother was. Arthur could feel him, almost as though he were alive again.

Arthur knelt at the foot of the grave, clasped his hands together, and bowed his head. The night wind rose up, and he heard the *hooty-hoot* of the owls and the staccato call of the katydids. And then Arthur heard *What's up, short stack?* Frank had called Arthur that, though Arthur was anything but short. It wasn't Frank's voice coming from his grave; it was his brother talking inside of him. But he heard him, clear as a bell.

"Gosh, Frank, I sure do miss you," Arthur said aloud.

I know you do.

"Do you miss us?"

Sure I do.

"Do you . . . see us?"

Course!

"I wish you'd appear."

I wish I could.

Arthur got quiet then. He guessed he was making this all up. Well, of course he was. And yet. Who knew what really happened when you died? Who knew how much truth there was in people saying they could communicate with the dead? If there were people who could do that, Arthur guessed he was one of them.

He closed his eyes, and whatever he was feeling grew richer and deeper. Then he opened his eyes, cleared his throat and said, "Guess what? I'm *still* only Nola's friend."

I know you're disappointed, saying that. But it's the best thing that could happen.

"I *love* her. You know that. It's not fake. It's not kid love. I want to marry her."

Your life is far from over, kid.

Oh, Arthur missed him bad then. He saw Frank in their bedroom, lying on his side in bed reading, furrows of concentration between his eyebrows. He saw him looking over at Arthur, a little amused. Not in a mean way, but in a way that made Arthur have hope, because whenever he looked at Arthur like that, some good advice inevitably followed.

Arthur got up and went to stand at the base of Frank's headstone. He picked up a handful of dirt and put it in his shirt pocket. He'd carry a bit of Frank along with him. As he felt Frank would carry him, always.

Chapter 25

ARTHUR GUESSED THERE were a lot of people who thought that time ought to hold still every now and then, out of respect for certain things. But it didn't, of course. Whatever happened on one day, good or bad, why, here came the next, and it put more distance between you and what you might have wanted to keep close for just a while longer.

So it was with Frank's death. Time passed, then passed some more, and then, just like that, it seemed, Arthur was in his senior year and Frank's death seemed forgotten. People didn't talk about him anymore. They weren't silent or tongue-tied around Arthur. He was back to being just another kid in high school.

Dead and gone; Arthur understood more than he wanted to what that meant now. Frank *was* gone. He'd been gloriously here, and now he was gone. On with the football games, the assemblies, the election of class officers and homecoming queens. On with the chilly or over-heated classrooms, the teachers droning on and on at their blackboards. And at home, on with life in a greatly diminished family, but a family nonetheless. Arthur's father was doing well in his work; the job he'd found seemed to suit him. His mother had adjusted to her husband being gone so often, and in fact Arthur thought she had come to enjoy her time alone. She joined a gardening club and the PTA, and she became a board member at the library. She did this last in Frank's honor, she said—he'd been the only real reader in the family. Arthur was keeping on with the Westerns Frank had introduced him to, but he knew his brother thought of those books as candy.

Arthur went regularly to Frank's grave. He could feel his brother there. And in their room, at night, Arthur lay in bed with his eyes closed, remembering how they'd whisper back and forth.

He was best friends with Nola, and that was both a heartbreak and a blessing. Every time they went somewhere together, which was every couple of weeks or so, Arthur hoped she would say, "Guess what? I'm through with all these dumb boys. I'm ready for a serious relationship with someone worthwhile, and that someone is you, Arthur Moses." He figured she'd use both his names in that instance. And he'd take her hands and say, "Nola Corrine McCollum, I have been waiting a long time to hear you say that." And she'd say, "I know, I just wasn't ready," and then she'd jump up a little and hug his neck and say, "I'm so happy!" He figured that's all it was, that she wasn't ready. He certainly didn't feel the need to tell her what must be obvious: that if she wanted him, he was all hers. He didn't want to put any pressure on her that way. He would bide his time. He didn't let himself think it would never happen.

One day in early May, only a few weeks from their graduation, Nola called and asked Arthur to meet her at what had become one of their favorite places: the band shell. When he arrived, she was already there, sitting on top of a picnic table and looking awfully blue. She had a letter in her hand.

When Arthur reached her, she handed him the letter, and he read it. She'd been accepted at St. Louis University.

He looked up at her, surprised. "I didn't know you wanted to go to college!"

"I didn't tell anybody."

"But you got in! Congratulations, Nola." That was what he said on the outside. Inside, he was saying, *Oh, no. Don't go.* "I'm really happy for you," he added.

"Thanks," she said, and then she burst into tears.

"What's wrong?" Arthur asked.

Nothing but more sobbing.

What was this? He sat beside her, and after a while he put his arm around her. He figured she'd either get angry and fling his arm off or she'd be grateful for the comfort, but either way, she'd stop crying.

That didn't happen. As soon as he put his arm around her, she leaned into his shoulder and kept on crying, louder.

Arthur just held her.

After a long while, Nola finally stopped crying. Arthur's arm was hurting, so he took it from around her and moved so that he was facing her. She was looking down and he wanted to see her eyes, so he lifted her chin ever so gently with his finger. That just set the blubbering off again, but the good part was that she lunged toward him and held him tightly. All kinds of things were taking the express elevator up his backbone.

Finally, Nola spoke, and she sounded like she had a bad cold.

"I'm so . . ." she said.

Arthur waited, and when she pulled away from him and spoke again, her voice had normalized. "I want to tell you something, Arthur, and I don't want anyone else to know."

"Okay." He'd had some experience with this.

"I'm ruined."

"You . . . What do you mean?"

She gave him a hard look. "I'm *ruined*!"

His face must have given away his lack of understanding.

"I had relations with someone."

"You did?"

She nodded miserably.

He wanted so badly to ask who; certain suspicions were parading in his brain, but he thought it was up to her if she wanted to tell him. He was aching inside, and all off-kilter, angry at her and whomever she'd been with, yet wanting only to make her feel better.

"Are you in the family way?" He'd had experience with this, too.

"No, it was only once, and it was six weeks ago. I'm not pregnant. But, oh, Arthur . . ." She began to cry again. "I'm so afraid he'll tell people. Or already has. When I look at everyone now, I wonder if they know. It seems like they're all looking at me differently."

"Has he admitted to telling anyone?"

She stared off into the woods. "I haven't been seeing him anymore. So I don't know."

"I guess it would depend on the character of the guy, whether he'd tell anyone else," Arthur said, hoping she'd make a revelation. "I haven't heard anything."

"I thought he had good character, but then . . . Oh, Arthur, I didn't want to do it. But we were out in the middle of nowhere in the back of his car and he just kept . . . And it happened so fast, he just . . . And then I started crying and he apologized, but it sure didn't seem like he meant it. Seemed like he was just proud of himself. I'm so ashamed! I don't know what to do."

"What do your girlfriends say?"

Her eyes widened. "I haven't told *them*! They'd tell everybody!"

"Was it Corky Daniels?" he asked. It just burst out of him.

"No, it wasn't anyone you know. He graduated from another school before his family moved here. His name is Binks. A nickname, for Benjamin."

An older man. The things Nola had been doing that he'd never known about! She was going out with older men while he had had a few dates with girls from their school. He'd tried dating Becky Reed again, but that experience put the kibosh on pursuing anything else with her. They'd gone to a basketball game at her request, and all she did was ogle Mike Osgood, who was captain of the team. She told Arthur how talented she thought Mike was, and asked him why was it that *he* never played any sports; wasn't there *anything* he could do, even just baseball? Tennis? Then, smiling, she said that maybe there should be a tiddlywinks team; would he like that? There was a fine line between gentle ribbing and disparagement, and Arthur knew the difference. He did something that night he wasn't proud of: he told Becky he was feeling sick—again!—and he walked out of the gymnasium and went home to read from one of his tree books. She knew her way home; she didn't need him to walk beside her while she offered her version of self-improvement for him. He doubted she'd care that he'd left. The next time he saw her, she stuck her nose up in the air and Arthur thought, *Fine.* He'd spend his time with Ann Woronowsky, who had a gentle nature and was going to be a nurse and seemed to appreciate him.

"I don't think I should go to college," Nola said.

"Because . . . ?"

She didn't answer. Arthur wondered if it was because of the way she thought she was ruined.

"Can I tell you something?" he asked her.

She nodded.

"I think it's wonderful that you got into college. Gosh, Nola, you're so smart and . . . capable! You're feeling bad right now, but you're going to be just fine, I know it. But if I can help you in any way, I will. I think you know that."

"But I never even wanted to go to college, Arthur! I just applied because my parents wanted me to. But I don't *want* to go. I always felt like . . . Well, I always felt like my destiny was for something else. Something *dazzling*. Isn't that dopey?"

"I don't think it's dopey at all," Arthur said. "And I believe in destiny."

"Do you?"

"I do. And Nola? If you don't want to go to college, I think you have every right not to. You have every right to decide what is best for you. Our lives . . . we have to make them for ourselves. We have to take chances on doing the things that mean the most to us." He sounded like Frank. He was glad he did.

Nola looked into his eyes for a long moment. Then she kissed his cheek—one, two, three times—and he nearly gasped with joy. She said, "You know what? Tonight, after dinner, I'm going to tell my parents I decided not to go to college. And I don't think they'll even be all that upset. They'll probably be relieved they don't need to take out a loan to pay my expenses! Let my little sister go; she's only in eighth grade, but she's *dying* to go to college. She wants to be the next Madame Curie. Oh, Arthur, thank you. I feel so relieved. And as for people in this town looking askance at me—"

"You let me know about anyone who bothers you and I'll punch them in the nose," Arthur said, flexing his non-muscles.

She smiled, and it was like the sun coming out.

"Okay?" Arthur said.

"Okay!" She hopped off the picnic table. "Want to walk? Will you tell me the names of things in the woods? I love it when you do that."

They set off together. Every tree they passed, Arthur named, and most of the flowers, too. Judging by Nola's reaction you would have thought *he* was Madame Curie.

After an hour or so the sun began setting, and Nola said, "I guess I'll go on home. But I just want to say . . . I just want to say I hope you don't think less of me, Arthur." Now her eyes filled with tears again.

"I couldn't think more of you, Nola. That will never change. It will *never* change." He reached out to gently wipe away tears that had spilled over onto her cheeks.

"Okay," she said. "Okay." She sniffed. "Gee, I think you're wonderful, Arthur. I hope you can see that." She stared so long at him he had to look away.

That night, Arthur sat at his desk and wrote a letter to Nola. The feelings he had for her had to go somewhere. If he couldn't say to her face how much he loved her, why, he'd let it all out on paper. But after he finished, he put the letter way in the back of his desk drawer. It came to him with a certainty he couldn't explain that someday he'd give it to her. But not now.

Chapter 26

ON SATURDAY MORNING, Arthur's family was having breakfast. It was french toast, which his dad had volunteered to make. What an event! His dad never cooked, and this french toast, burned on one side and raw on the other, proved it. But Arthur and his mother drowned their servings in maple syrup and congratulated the chef, who sat behind his newspaper, knowing full well that what he'd made was not up to par, but peeking over the top of the pages every now and then to solicit more appreciation.

Just as they finished eating, the phone rang, and they all looked at one another, surprised. Nine o'clock was not terribly early, but it wasn't a time when people usually called on the weekend.

His mother answered the phone a little anxiously. Then she smiled and lay her hand across her chest. She said, "Not at all. I'm so glad you called. Please come right over. Do you know the address?"

While she gave directions, Arthur and his father exchanged glances. Arthur thought they both were wondering the same thing.

Arthur's mother sat back down and said, "Guess who's coming over to visit?"

"Who?" his father asked.

"Your grandson."

His dad opened his mouth, then closed it. Arthur sat still as a stone, then ran up to his room to see if there was anything he could give a baby. He'd never made the trip out to visit Mary, but she had written to him after the baby was born, telling Arthur she'd had a boy, and that she'd named him Frank. Also, she'd gotten married to another teacher; he was a wonderful man named Wendell Hayes, an art teacher whom she hoped Arthur would meet one day. Wendell was crazy about little Frank, she said.

"Hayes," Arthur had whispered to himself, after he'd read that. It bothered him that Frank's child would not have Frank's last name. But he would have a father.

Arthur had shared the letter with his parents, and neither of them had said anything. It was one of those times when no words said all of them.

But today they would see Frank's baby. Arthur knew that each of them was nervous for various reasons, but he knew, too, that they were all glad Mary was coming.

Frank was the first one through the door. He was almost two years old now, and had such an air of exuberance about him that Arthur couldn't stop smiling at him. He was wearing yellow corduroy overalls, a striped

T-shirt, and a navy-blue cardigan. He had bells tied onto his baby shoes. Arthur figured that was so Mary could keep track of him: he was a very busy boy. He walked around touching everything in the kitchen, then went on into the living room. Mary apologized, laughing, saying, "He has no fear." She, Arthur's mother, and Arthur went after the toddler, an impromptu game of follow-the-leader. Arthur's father and Wendell stayed in the kitchen—being men, Arthur guessed, or maybe his father wanted to give his wife time alone with Frank's child. But Arthur was mesmerized by the boy.

At one point, Arthur lifted Frank up onto his lap and pulled out of his back pocket the little book of poetry he'd taken from the bookshelf in his bedroom. He opened it to "Birches," with its beautiful illustration of the leaning trees. Mary and his mother were engaged in conversation, so he could tell Frank privately, "You see this? Your father loved this poem. Someday, I think you will, too." The boy lunged at the book and Arthur feared he would tear the page. But he didn't. He only wanted to see closer. He sat still then, just looking, his small hand splayed on the page. Arthur could see the dimples above every knuckle. He could hear the boy's rapid breathing. He could smell the top of his head, a kind of salty life smell. It was all Arthur could do not to squeeze him and squeeze him and squeeze him.

After a while, Frank wanted down and Arthur gave the book to Mary, saying, "My brother loved this book. I want Frank to have it."

She took it from him and looked at the cover. "I gave this to him," she said, and her voice was awfully unreliable-sounding. She told Arthur, "Thank you so much for this. I'll read it to him as soon as he can understand. He'll love it, I know he will. Already he pays such attention to everything, just as Frank always did."

Arthur nodded, his hands shoved deep into his pockets.

Mary and Wendell were on their way to visit his parents, and they didn't stay much longer. But after Arthur and his parents waved goodbye to them, his dad said, "We'll see them again." Arthur thought so, too.

He saw Nola after school on Monday, surrounded by her usual bunch of friends. She was back to being herself, and Arthur was glad. He asked if he could have a word with her. "Sure!" she said. "See you tomorrow!" she called to her friends. "Will you walk me home?" she asked, and Arthur said, "Of course."

"Something really swell happened on Saturday," Arthur said.

"What?" Nola asked, but she was staring down at the sidewalk, avoiding cracks. She still did that.

"I met Frank's baby."

Nola stopped walking. She burst into tears. Then she started laughing, saying, "I have no idea why I'm crying."

Arthur thought he did.

"Tell me everything!" she said. "Does he look like Frank?"

Arthur did tell her everything, including the fact that

he thought the baby *did* look like Frank: his wide blue eyes, the dimple in his chin. It seemed like Nola would always be the one he wanted to tell things to. He thought, *If you have someone in your life like that, someone you know you will always want to tell everything to, you are awfully lucky, and a fool to ask for more.* But, of course, he was a fool.

Chapter 27

A FTER GRADUATION, NOLA got a job working as a secretary at the telephone company. Arthur got a job at
a nursery. They still spent time together every now and
then, but it was different now.

When they got together, they talked about their bosses,
the people they worked with, ways they hoped they might
advance. They didn't talk much about the people they
dated; it was easy to see neither of them was doing well in
that department. "Anyone new in your life?" Nola might
ask, and Arthur would say yes and tell her who it was, or
he'd say no, he was still with whomever he was seeing at
the time. "How's it going with Riley?" Arthur might ask,
and Nola would say, "It's Allen, now."

Arthur just couldn't figure it out; it seemed to him that
a beautiful girl like Nola would have her pick of any of the
men in town. Frankly, he was surprised she hadn't gotten
married yet. Though it was true that this last fellow she
was seeing, a flashy car salesman, didn't seem to be mar-

riage material. Arthur didn't want to come right out and say it, but he thought the guy was careless with her. Frank used to say it was bad when girls thought you were too nice, but didn't they chafe against a guy who showed up late to take you out, who borrowed money from you when he came up short and then never paid it back? Also, he'd seen this Walter walking around town with another girl, and at one point he had pushed her up against a storefront and kissed her. Arthur had wanted to tell Nola about that, but he'd learned that sometimes when you tried to help you could make things worse. If he spoke out against Walter, Nola might double down in her affection for him: love made people do funny things. He figured she'd see him for what he was soon enough.

One day, when the magnolia blossoms were primed for blooming, Nola called and asked Arthur to meet her after work, by the river. He was the first to arrive, and he sat on the bank and removed his shoes and socks and rolled up his trouser legs. He had still never revealed his feet to Nola, but today was going to be the day. He stepped gingerly into the cold water but made a hasty retreat and put his socks back on, then his shoes. Let Nola do her wading to her heart's content. He'd be her audience. As usual.

He leaned back on his hands and looked around. It was so peaceful here, like an outdoor church. All the green and growing things, all the life you could see, and all the life that was hidden from you but there nonetheless. He remembered Mrs. Crawford talking about the comfort she found being outside and working in her garden. He wished she weren't moving, but ever since her husband died, she hadn't been the same. Last time he walked past her house and talked to her over the fence, she'd told him she would be selling her house soon. "Maybe you should buy it," she'd said. "You're the only one who would take care of my roses properly."

"I wish I could," Arthur said, and he did, with all his heart. But he'd never be able to afford it. "Rest assured, I'll keep after whoever does buy it."

She nodded, smiling, and then suddenly became tearful. "You're a pleasure to know, Arthur."

"Well. Thank you. You are, too!"

"You've become such a fine young man. You're someone I'll miss."

"I'll miss you, too. I heard you were moving out east. Charleston, someone said."

"Yes, I've got a sister there. Much as I love Mason, I need a bit of a fresh start. I hope I'll like it there."

"You know what they say," Arthur had said. "The people who like where they're living generally like a new place, too. I predict you'll be very happy there."

Arthur looked at his watch. Nola was late. He hoped she hadn't forgotten, but she never had yet.

And then there she was, dressed in a nice turquoise dress, a scarf around her neck. "Hi," she said, plopping down beside him on the riverbank.

"I tried wading," Arthur said. "Didn't work out so well."

"Oh?" Her voice was listless. Arthur had thought she'd

tear off her shoes and say something like "Let an expert show you how!" but she barely responded at all.

"Are you going in?" Arthur asked.

"In where?"

Arthur pointed to the river.

"Oh. No. Not today. Or ever again, probably."

His heart began to race. Was she sick? He wasn't a religious man, but he became one in that instant and offered up a prayer against the possibility of any illness. "Are you okay?" he asked. She nodded.

It was quiet for a while, then. Arthur thought about how comfortable it was when silence fell between them. With other women, when the talking stalled, the space was immediately filled with a rush of meaningless yakkity-yak. Nola was the only woman he knew who understood the value of just keeping still, of letting conversation happen in a natural way. And, anyway, in the silences that he and Nola shared, they were still talking. More than once, they'd even looked over and smiled at each other at the same moment, when not a word had been spoken. He liked to believe it was because they shared a communication deeper than common conversation. He looked at the river moving slowly by and he thought: *Like that. Like the current.*

Finally, Nola said, "Arthur? I have to tell you something."

Hope rose in him; would it *ever* stop?

"I'm moving to St. Louis."

He felt like he'd been socked in the gut. "You are?"

"Yes."

"When?"

"Tomorrow. I'm taking the six-fourteen evening train."

"So sudden!"

"Not really. I've been thinking about it a lot. I just wanted to make the decision by myself, without anyone else's opinion. So . . ."

So? Arthur thought.

She looked over at him and smiled sadly, shook her head. "I don't feel like I can stay in this town. I feel like it's all played out for me. I have no great job prospects. And I have no one who . . ."

She became brisk and businesslike. "My prospects in St. Louis will be better all around. I think at heart I'm a big-city woman, not a small-town one."

Arthur couldn't speak. He nodded, trying to keep the misery from his face.

"I think I'll really like all the hustle and bustle. All the things to *do*."

"Yeah, sure," he managed.

"Maybe you'll come and visit me? If you're not . . . if you're free?"

"That would be something, huh?"

"You'd like St. Louis, I'll bet."

He wanted to say sure he would, but it would have been a lie. And so he told her the truth. "I don't like big cities, Nola. They make me kind of nervous. So much to pay attention to. So much . . . everything. Frank used to make fun of me for liking it here so much; he wanted to move to New York City, which is the Godzilla of cities. But I like it here. I *love* it here. Maybe I'm just a simpleton."

"Oh, no!" Nola cried. "You're not a simpleton.

You're . . ." She began to cry and Arthur, bewildered, reached in his pocket for his handkerchief and gave it to her.

"Thank you," she said, embarrassed. "I'm just kind of emotional. I guess moving is a bigger deal than I thought." She wiped at her eyes, her nose, then sat up straight. "But I'm going; I'm going to get on that train and I'm going to go. I have a reservation at a hotel for a week, and during that time I'm going to find a job and an apartment, maybe with a roommate I could be friends with. I have to try, or I'll just . . ." She looked over at him, her eyes filling again. "Do you understand?"

It was hard to answer. He took his time. Then he took her hands into his, probably for the last time. And he said, "I believe in you, Nola."

"Well, that just means everything," she said. "And I believe in you, too."

"Okay," he said. "Nola? Can I take you to the station tomorrow?"

"Oh, that's so nice of you to offer. Thank you, Arthur."

"I'll come by right after work."

"Okay." She smiled. "Gosh. I'm excited now! I was so blue when I came to tell you, but now I'm excited. I'm moving to St. Louis!"

"Yup," he said.

He'd wear his best suit. She'd see him that way and reconsider. She'd say, "Arthur, I've changed my mind. And since you're wearing that nice suit and I'm wearing my nice suit, let's go and get married."

Or he'd help her up the metal steps onto the train car,

then watch her for as long as he could while she made her way down the aisle. And then the train would pull away.

In fact, that was exactly what happened the next day. Before Nola boarded, he told her there wasn't a doubt in his mind that she would be a big success. Why, she'd probably get famous or something. Her excitement in hearing that made her rise up on her toes and say, "Oh, Arthur, wouldn't that be *some*thing?"

He reached inside his jacket for a gift he'd gotten her: a bouquet of silk violets, tied with a blue ribbon. At least that would last.

"Oh, my," she said when he put the bouquet in her hand. "How beautiful." She swallowed hard and looked up at him, Nola with her clear blue eyes. "Can I ask you something, Arthur? Am I doing the right thing?"

He stood still. He couldn't speak for fear of saying something wrong. Or of crying! In his head was only this: *Nola. Nola. Nola.*

But then she stepped back from him, and Nola's voice was stronger. She said, "I'll keep this by my bedside, and I'll look at it every night."

"Boooooarrrrrd!" they heard, and Arthur took Nola's elbow and helped her up the steps to the train.

At the top of the stairs, she turned. For a long moment, she said nothing. But then more passengers lined up to get on the train and she said, "Well. Okay, then. Bye, Arthur."

And he said, "Bye, Nola."

She disappeared into the train car, and Arthur wondered who would sit by her, and he wondered if whoever it was would have any idea how wonderful she was.

After the train was out of sight, Arthur didn't know what to do. And so he walked. When he came to the wide-open field at the outskirts of town, he started for a stand of trees at the center.

What now?

He wasn't a boy any longer. He was man now, a fact that still snuck up on him sometimes. But he *was* a man, changed in nearly all ways from boyhood, except for still being smitten with the same girl he'd loved since he was sixteen years old. It didn't seem that his affections would ever wander, and he guessed he didn't want them to.

He was above all a man who made himself content with his circumstances. He had known the hammer of misfortune, and he knew as well the salvation that could follow. He lived in a small town undistinguished in every way, but it did not occur to him to leave it. He grew in the direction of warmth, and it seemed to him that Mason was his sun.

He took off his suit jacket, folded it carefully in half, and draped it over a low branch of a cottonwood tree. He sat down, crossed his arms over his knees, and waited. Here came the sideways flight and metallic glint of a dragonfly as it lit here and there in the tall weeds, then settled.

Would everything eventually work out, one way or another? He guessed he'd see. In the meantime, he sat beneath the blue sky, smelled the tall green grasses, watched the forming and reforming clouds and the leaves moving in the wind, and he listened to the call of the birds who sang the song he liked best: *Here! Here! Here!*

Chapter 28

ALMOST A YEAR later, on a beautiful spring day, Arthur's mother was sitting out on the back steps in the golden light of late afternoon, embroidering a dresser scarf for little Frank's bedroom. Arthur stood inside, leaning against the doorframe, his arms crossed, watching her for a while. It seemed to him that there was something so lovely about women using their hands for such work. If he were a painter, here would be his subject.

Arthur came out the door, and his mother looked up at him and smiled.

"How was work?" she asked.

Arthur sat down beside her and showed her his hands. "Dirty," he said. "But good. Old man Snelling told me today he's going to be selling the nursery. Says he's too old to keep up with it. Asked me if I wanted to buy it."

"Really?"

"Yup."

"So what do you think?"

Arthur shrugged. "I guess it would be all right. But Harvey Guldorp told me there was a job opening soon in the Parks Department, and I think I'd rather apply for that. I'd like to be outside all day and get paid for it."

"Harvey knows all the scuttlebutt."

"Well, that's one thing being assistant to the mayor of this town is good for. But he always did know what was going on, even when we were in high school. His nickname was Ferret, remember?"

His mother smiled. "I do remember that. And a parks job sounds perfect for you. It would be a good, stable job. The parks aren't going anywhere!"

"Ma? I decided to buy Mrs. Crawford's old house."

"Arthur! Did you really? I saw the For Sale sign just yesterday. I guess it didn't work out for the new people, huh?"

"Well, I talked to them. They were out in the yard, pruning the roses the wrong way. I told them I'd always wanted to buy that house and they gave me their real estate agent's name. So tomorrow I'm going to make an offer. I've got enough saved for the down payment."

"Well, this is just wonderful news! Good for you, son! And you know your father and I will help if you need it."

"I think I'll be okay. But thanks."

"You'll be a homeowner!" his mother said. And then, "So how was your date last night? With . . . Emily, was it?"

"Yes. Emily Richards."

"She seems like a nice girl. You've seen her quite a few times now. Is it serious?" Her tone was careful.

Arthur thought he knew what she was aiming at. It seemed like everyone he knew was in a serious relationship, even engaged or married. And now here he was buying a house. His mother probably hoped he was going to make an announcement.

"She's a nice girl," Arthur said. Then he sighed and told his mother about all the women he'd been seeing, Emily included: mild-mannered women who placed their dinner napkins on their laps just so; women who invited him to their places for dinner with hopeful expressions on their faces when he arrived, and disappointed ones when he left. One of them had presented him with a quivering aspic for an appetizer that brought back something Frank had told him long ago: *If ever a woman serves you aspic, run for the hills.* His mother laughed when he told her that.

It probably wasn't true, what Frank implied, but it was irrelevant, anyway. Arthur's heart had been given away long ago to a girl who went barefoot at the first sign of spring, and who had left Mason almost a year ago that day. Apart from a few neutral postcards he'd gotten after she'd first arrived in St. Louis, she hadn't written to him. Arthur guessed she was busy with her new life, and he didn't want to hound her, sending her letters about goings-on in a town she'd been eager to get away from.

He had tried so hard to get Nola out of his head and to find someone else, but it just didn't work. He figured he'd be one of those lifelong bachelors who turned funny. But at least he'd turn funny in a fine house.

He said, "I'll tell you the truth, Ma, which you probably know anyway. I'm still in love with Nola McCollum; that's why it doesn't work with these other women. And the idea of being with Nola is hopeless."

"No it isn't," his mother said.

"For Pete's sake, Ma, you know I don't have a chance with her. I never did!"

His mother looked up from her embroidery. "I don't know any such thing. I don't believe I've ever met anyone as kind as you, Arthur. Don't you think that's worth something?"

"Not for this kind of thing."

"What kind of thing? Tell me exactly what you mean."

"Well, I wanted to *marry* her, Ma! Besides that, she's in St. Louis. I'm never going to live in St. Louis!"

His mother tied off a stitch and clipped it with her embroidery scissors. Then she turned to Arthur and spoke quietly. "Nola is not in St. Louis. I saw Sandy Michaels at the beauty parlor yesterday and she told me Nola had moved back to Mason. I didn't tell you right away because I didn't know if you and Emily . . . I wasn't sure I should say."

Arthur felt light-headed. "Are you sure she's not just visiting?"

"Nola's mom told Sandy she's back to stay. She got here a few days ago. She's staying with her parents for now. She tried to get her old job here back, but there was nothing for her. So now she's looking for something else."

"Gosh," Arthur said, in a voice barely audible, even to himself.

"Gosh," his mother agreed.

"I don't know what to do," Arthur said.

"It will come to you. You have time." She looked at her watch. "Say, would you do me a favor? I'm all out of envelopes and I've got to mail some letters. Would you go to the dime store and buy me some before dinner? Then I can get them addressed and you can mail them on your way to work tomorrow."

"Sure. I need some things, too."

The whole way to the store Arthur kept an eye out for Nola. It was unlikely that he'd see her, but not impossible. At the dime store he bought his mother her envelopes and then for the life of him could not remember what he needed. He ended up choosing only a bag of salted nuts and was heading for the cashier when Nola walked in. She'd lost weight and she looked tired, nothing like the lively girl who had gone off to the big city with such high hopes. She didn't see Arthur, just headed toward the back of the store where the parakeets were kept. He followed her there and stood watching as she spoke gently to the birds, her forehead resting against the cage.

"Nola?" he said, and she spun around, her hand on her chest.

"Arthur! Oh my gosh, how *are* you?" She laughed and pointed to the birds. "I'm just chatting with my friends here."

Arthur looked at the cage, at the confusion of colors and feathers and noise. Birds flew all over the place, and many seemed to be fighting for a place on the swing, which would hold only one bird.

"I'm glad you're back," Arthur said.

She nodded, and her eyes filled with tears. "Oh, Arthur, you don't know how much I . . . I wrote you so many letters I never sent you."

"You did?"

She nodded.

"Why didn't you send them?"

"Oh, I don't know. I guess I was embarrassed at first, and then it seemed like too much time had passed for me to suddenly . . ."

"What were you embarrassed about?"

Nola stared into the birdcage to answer him. "For one thing, nothing was working out. The truth is, I regretted leaving here the moment I got on the train. I didn't really want to go. I just didn't know what else to do."

"*I* sure didn't want you to go!"

She spun around. "But you were so *encouraging* of me doing it!" Her voice was a little loud; a customer passing by in the next aisle looked disapprovingly at them.

Arthur moved closer to Nola and spoke softly. "Only because I thought it was what *you* wanted. I didn't want to hold you up from realizing your dreams."

"St. Louis was more like a nightmare. It felt just . . . *frantic* there! I called my mother the second night I was there, telling her I wanted to come home. She said I owed it to myself to stay there for a year, that of *course* I was homesick now. Things would get better, she said. Only they didn't. Mostly what I did there was think about all the mistakes I'd made in my life and feel terrible."

"I sure am sorry you felt that way," Arthur said. He hesitated, then added, "But *everybody* makes mistakes, Nola. To think you won't, or can't, why, *that's* a mistake! It's what you do *after* the mistake that counts most."

"Well," Nola said, raising her chin to look him in the eye, "that's why I'm back here. I realized more and more what Mason meant to me. And you. I missed so much being with you, talking to you. I wrote to you like a diary."

"What did you tell me?"

She smiled. "Oh, silly things. What I did that day. Things I saw on the street. What I had for *dinner*. I told you about people I worked with. And . . . I told you how much I missed you, Arthur. Gosh. I missed you an awful lot."

Arthur frowned and put his hands in his pockets. "I sure wish you'd sent those letters. I would have written back to you lickety-split. Way it was, I didn't want to disturb you."

"Well, I still have them. Maybe someday I'll give them to you."

"I have a letter I never gave you, either," he said. He leaned in closer to her. "When you give me yours, I'll give you mine."

"Oh, Arthur, weren't we foolish?" She put her hand on his arm so lightly he could barely feel it. "Do you think . . . Could we be together again, like before?"

Inside the birdcage was a great deal of squawking as

the birds fought for the swing. A small green bird, not the showiest of the bunch, not an elegant gray or turquoise blue or silvery white, but just a common green one, flew up to the side of the swing and hung on to it, upside down. For a moment, it looked like he would fall, but then he grabbed on to the perch, pulled himself up, and stayed there.

"Could we be together like before?" Arthur said. "Hmmm. Well, I have to say . . . Nope, I don't think we can be."

Nola pulled her hand away and pressed her lips together. She looked close to tears again. "I understand. I didn't even ask if you . . . You're probably involved with—"

"Reason is, I think a husband and wife are more than friends. And I am going to marry you, Nola."

She froze. Then she said, *"When?"*

Arthur told this story many times, but never to the one with whom he wanted most to share it. Oh, he told Frank. He stood at the foot of his grave, and he spoke the words out loud to him. But that was the time, out of all the times Arthur talked to him, that he wished hardest to hear his brother's voice, whispering back to him, *Shazam! What'd I tell you?*

Mason, Missouri
Winter 2016

EVERY NOW AND then a bird flies across the window, and it reminds Arthur of something he can't say. Can't put into words. Frank would have been the one to do that.

He has been watching home movies play out in his brain, and he wonders now what persuades people to a certain point of view about their own lives. Is it a person? A place? An incident?

It makes no difference, really. In the end, you are left only with your own soul's generosity, your own heart's love, and it is given to you to understand what was spent and what was not.

Arthur closes his eyes. Oh, he was a lucky man. He still is.

The birds fly off to who knows where—that's what he means to say. They fly off to who knows where and they don't look back. And in the spring, there are the new ones, their mouths wide open.

Acknowledgments

It is very rare—almost never, really—that I take suggestions from someone about what to write. I need to follow my own impulses; and I also worry that if I take a suggestion from someone else, I will have to live up to their expectations. An exception was my novel *We Are All Welcome Here,* which was written at a suggestion of a woman who wanted me to tell her mother's story. All it took was for me to see a photograph of that woman, and to hear from her daughter that I could do whatever I wanted, and I was in.

Earth's the Right Place for Love came at the suggestion of my brilliant editor, Kate Medina, who told me she wanted to know how Arthur Moses, the main character in *The Story of Arthur Truluv,* came to be the man he was. As it happened, I wanted to know that, too. It occurred to me that sometimes tragedy can bring a person to great humanity. I knew almost immediately what that tragedy would be for Arthur: an incident that occurs when he is sixteen. What I didn't know was how much the love story that is also in the book would come to have the dominant place that it did. Given the state of the world, I'm glad I got to focus on the worth of love. Thank you, Kate, for intuiting what would be a good book for me to write next, and for all your suggestions that helped make the book better. Thank you also for your *you*-ness: Since the day we first met, I have pretty much adored you. And you pick the best assistants! I will very much miss Noa Shapiro, but look forward to working with Louisa McCollough, who already has demonstrated how fine *she* is.

I also want to thank my agent, Suzanne Gluck, who's as smart and capable—and fun!—as they come, and Beth Pearson, who copyedited this book with great sensitivity and insight. Beth is a dream to work with, and I hope she will be there for any future books that I write.

Others I would like to thank for their excellent work include my publicist, Melissa Folds, and Madison Dettlinger, who is a marketing guru and model of patience for certain authors who are constantly befuddled by Facebook, not to say any aspect of technology.

Thanks to managing editor Rebecca Berlant, production manager Erin Korenko, and production editor Jennifer Rodriguez. And a very special shoutout to Ella Laytham and Greg Mollica, who designed the beautiful cover for this book. This jacket is proof positive that an image can speak louder than words. It says everything I could have hoped for about what this novel is trying to convey.

The gifted women in my writing groups were, as usual, with me all the way: Thanks to Lee and Betsy Woodman, Donna Stein, Mary Mitchell, Jessica Treadway, Marja Mills, Julie Bolton, and Julia Keller.

My talented and honest writer and artist friend Phyllis Florin took time away from her own work to weigh in on pages from this novel. My dogs, Austin and Gabby, provided comfort and diversion. And Murphy, you know what you did and do, but I hope never to stop expressing my appreciation for all that you are to me.

ABOUT THE AUTHOR

ELIZABETH BERG is the author of many bestselling novels, including *The Story of Arthur Truluv, Night of Miracles, The Confession Club, Open House* (an Oprah's Book Club selection), *Talk Before Sleep,* and *The Year of Pleasures,* as well as the short story collection *The Day I Ate Whatever I Wanted. Durable Goods* and *Joy School* were selected as ALA Best Books of the Year. She adapted her novel *The Pull of the Moon* into a play that enjoyed sold-out performances in Chicago and Indianapolis. Berg's work has been published in thirty-one countries, and three of her novels have been turned into television movies. She is the founder of Writing Matters, a reading series dedicated to serving author, audience, and community. She teaches writing workshops and is a popular speaker at venues around the country. Some of her most popular Facebook postings have been collected in *Make Someone Happy, Still Happy,* and *Happy to Be Here.* Elizabeth Berg lives outside Chicago with her excellent dogs.

elizabeth-berg.net
Facebook.com/bergbooks

ABOUT THE TYPE

This book was set in Sabon, a typeface designed by the well-known German typographer Jan Tschichold (1902–74). Sabon's design is based upon the original letterforms of sixteenth-century French type designer Claude Garamond and was created specifically to be used for three sources: foundry type for hand composition, Linotype, and Monotype. Tschichold named his typeface for the famous Frankfurt typefounder Jacques Sabon (c. 1520–80).